Born in Beirut in 1964, Tony Ha..... up in the Lebanon and educated at Winchester anu the Warburg Institute where he read Renaissance Studies. He has worked for Sotheby's in Madrid and at the Tate Gallery. He now lives in West London.

HOMESICK

TONY HANANIA

BLOOMSBURY

First published in Great Britain 1997

This paperback edition published 1998

Copyright © 1997 by Tony Hanania

The moral right of the author has been asserted
Bloomsbury Publishing Plc, 38 Soho Square, London W1V 5DF

A CIP catalogue record for this book is available from the British Library

ISBN 07475 3497 7

Typeset in Great Britain by Hewer Text Composition Services,
Edinburgh
Printed in Great Britain by Clays Limited, St Ives plc

History, like childhood, is not the memory of a unity that never existed, but the awareness of a precarious condition of falling that has never ceased to prevail.

Paul de Man

What we found inside the Palestinian Chatila camp at ten o'clock on the morning of 18 September 1982 did not quite beggar description, although it would have been easier to re-tell in the cold prose of a medical examination . . . We questioned the survivors again. We heard strange stories. Foley was told that an Israeli photographer believed one of the massacre victims had been a Jewish holocaust survivor . . . The woman had married an Arab, travelling into exile with him in 1948 and eventually settling in the slums of Chatila. Foley did not see the photographer again. We could never confirm the story.

Robert Fisk

CONTENTS

Prelude

Leaving town had been the usual obstacle course, all the masked messengers and speed humps and concussive slogans on the hoardings along the way David had chosen to give us at least the illusion of progress, but it was still light when we reached the motorway, if you can call that light. Though there was space ahead the traffic was staying clotted together, like clutches of a tune timid of breaking away into noise.

Out into the country the familiar syntax of the road worked its gentle hypnoticism. The undiverting overpasses, junctions, signs to unvisited towns, *Farnborough*, *Fleet*, *Farnham*, the fields still heavy with hoar-frost: of course this was the same. Only the traffic had changed. Sleeker, slower, all homomorphic now. It's what I would have seen coming back from Terminal 3 if I had bothered to look out. But usually I was too interested in the car to notice much outside. We were always met in a different sports car, when my father, stopping off on his way to the States where he was lecturing on Middle East Affairs, had chosen to accompany me back to school. An MGB, a Stag, even an E-type once. I suppose there were different women though I only remember one. Somewhere between Jackie O. and Coco Chanel: a curdled looker under a topical bob, and always the same slightly pained expression. I would be scrunched up on the back ledge with my Gladstone bag, peering down at the glowing dashboard, its lights reflected back in the patent blackness of her boots and out above the viscous sheen of the road. The car would be full of sickly expensive scent, mixing with that coffee and damp camelhair smell which my father took with him when travelling. By the time we reached the school all the other boys would be in bed. While the woman stayed a few paces back I would press my nose deep into his cashmere belly, standing outside the pointed arch in the dark. Later I would be enraged that there had been nobody up to see the sports car. For who would entirely believe me now when I described its finer points?

As we passed the Fleet turning David switched on the radio. There were cover versions of cover versions . . . *and your heart was an open book you used to sa-ay* . . . Nothing we liked, but he left it playing low anyway, blending in with the road purr. It relieved us from having to talk for a while.

Having already been conceded my one in-car smoke I kept my fingers busy with one of Sammy's SuperHeroes which had been squidged under the console. The thing was part humanoid, part reptile, part robot. I wanted to ask David if he had bought it on request or on spec. He kept looking down to see what I was doing. Perhaps he was worried I was going to break it. Maybe he didn't even recognize the thing. Normally this was Rachel's car. She did the school runs and the shopping runs in it: Rachel with her pasteurized skin and post-historical gaze, queen of the gene-pool. This was a capsule built to protect the future, a life hearse. And I felt reproached by it; whenever I returned now it was as a shabby tourist around my friends' protected breeding programmes and their bloodless dinner-tables.

All winter the country has been giving back its dead. The rains

4

have uncovered more shallow graves on the pine terraces of Sanine and in the deserted wadis of the Chouf, corpses from the camp massacres coming up under the rough and the bunkers of the Golf Club in the places where the rings of birds gathered, and through the sands below the ruined villas of Damour and Tyre, their bone wrists and ankles still secured with plastic cuffs and rotting ropes; for the most part they were without denomination, without nationality, unclaimable. The old city is surfacing too: Roman, Greek, Phoenician remains, showing up through the shelled-out ruins around Martyrs' Square which are being dynamited away now to make way for the new trade city. And from every part of the city the people come, and from Jounieh and the south and down from the mountains to stare at these densely pitted stumps around the square, a petrified lava of infinite suggestion, as fantastical as the volcanic islands of Max Ernst.

The sky was losing its remaining light. David had relaxed now that I had put down the SuperHero. He kept his eyes on the tail-lights ahead. It was easier driving like that, following lights, not having to judge the distance. As he turned the radio down he sniffed the air, as one does at the beginning of a walk.

'I never used to come down this way.'

'No.'

'I'd would come with the others, on the train from Waterloo.'

'Better that way.'

David was scanning the Embankment and the signs, his shoulders hunching up again. He was determined not to miss the turning.

Part One

recon by fire

Wherever we were my mother would recite me lines she had been taught by the nuns before I went to sleep. Her voice would be hushed and confidential, as if she was afraid of being overheard:

> *Partant pour la Syrie le jeune et beau Dunois*
> *Venait prier Marie de bénir ses exploits.*
> *'Faites, Reine Immortelle,' lui dit-il en partant,*
> *'Que j'aime la plus belle et sois le plus vaillant.'*

This was one of her favourites, and when she missed out verses I would know that she had a lot of getting ready to do that evening and I would lie in wait behind my door to watch her pass down the corridor in her long strapless dress.

Sometimes I woke to find myself in a strange hotel room and I would go down to ask the concierge if he knew where my parents had gone. The last time was in Seville during August. I ran out into the streets in my Ladybird pyjamas and soon discovered them in a little square filled with orange trees, eating melon balls with ham that stretched like Plasticine and was as difficult to swallow. When the summer was over I was presented with a set of knights on horseback, some jousting, others waving spiked balls on chains, which I had been secretly hoping to receive for my eighth birthday back in July when we had spent every day at the beach in windy Portugal and the end of summer had seemed so remote that I still half-believed it would never come. Although I did not have time to stage a full tournament with the knights, I had decided to entrust them to the care of my parents when they left. They seemed a little surprised about this, and reluctant to take back the box, but I insisted.

All the *new men*, as we were called, along with a few senior boys, were housed in a long attic dormitory known as St Cross. It was a bare and cold place with nothing on the walls and curtains like J-Cloths which nobody bothered to close because they were so thin. There were no carpets on the floorboards over which a glutinous patina of polish preserved ancient marks and stains like insects framed in amber. I found my name (correctly spelt) stuck to one of the fifteen iron beds at right-angles to the empty walls, the type with jigsaw joints holding the head and foot to the frame, and thick wire mesh supporting a lumpy mattress. I was between 'Palgrave' and 'Standish', both of whom were curled up doggo under their tartan rugs.

Between the beds there were squat chests with four drawers, heavily emulsioned over. Most of the original drawer-knobs had been replaced with miscellaneous iron clasps and transparent plastic rosettes. On top of these chests boys had placed the contents of their sponge-bags (shampoo, toothpaste and brush in a plastic mug, hairbrush and comb), along with a four-by-six of the parents in a leather frame, though a few were in silver. Bears were also on the clothes list but several of the new men had brought along other familiars. My neighbour Standish was clasping what appeared to be a racoon with advanced alopecia, ancestral by the smell of it, and the boy beyond had brought a Scotty and a badger with a long black snout.

I had watched this boy earlier in the evening attempt to fasten a poster above his bed. He had been unable to stretch high enough to secure the top of the poster, which would adhere for a moment before springing back off the wall. On the other side of the room an older boy with bushy red hair had been watching this while reclining on his bed. With much perseverance the boy with the badger had finally made the poster stick. After he had stepped back gingerly to admire his handiwork, the older boy had strolled over, stretched effortlessly up to the poster, untacked it, and carefully rolled it into a tidy tube, patting down the edges with his open palms. Without even glancing back at the owner of the badger who looked on forlornly, the older boy raised the tube to his lips, blew a couple of rasping notes, and then loped slowly back to his bed from where he languidly surveyed the room through his new telescope, as if it were all some battle far out to sea.

Later that night I had been awakened by the sounds of a struggle. Some of the lights had been switched on again. Three of the older boys were on the floor wrestling for what appeared to be one of the drawers with wooden knobs. This confirmed my worst suspicions. I had been abandoned in a wild and savage place. My parents had privily divined my nature and chosen to throw me back among my own kind.

I lay on my bed staring up at the rib-cage of exposed roof beams. From somewhere far beneath me in the inner recesses of the building there came a faint pounding, like the heart of something trapped. On windless nights I would lie awake picturing vast broken wings, a chained colossus, undying organisms buried in stone.

This name St Cross had already caught in my throat, a bolus of something that mustn't be swallowed. For weeks to come this name would exercise me, this name which I sensed contained violence of a different order from anything that could come across from the other side of the room . . . I had seen the dragon's footprints in the bay beside the old port, near the little chapel where people left their old gloves, shoes, boots, though never in pairs. I had seen the remains of the pillar on which our saint had sat for twenty years, a giant egg out in the middle of the desert, eroded by the nails of pilgrims. I knew that as saints go these two had got off lightly. Perhaps St Cross had not been so fortunate. Although saints carried crosses they all had names as well, simple names, like George and Simon. Again and again, I tried to imagine, and I tried not to imagine, what had to have happened to someone for them to lose their own name.

The following morning I was woken by the incessant cooing of pigeons under the eaves. Boys were already shuffling off through the pewter light towards the wash-rooms in their old men dressing-gowns. When I came back from washing my neighbour Standish was sitting at the end of his bed in his grey flannel shorts and herring-bone tweed jacket (only the seniors were allowed to wear long trousers), struggling to knot his tie, and pretending not to blub. I dressed quickly, unused to the cold, and followed the other boys down the stone steps and long corridors to the brightly lit refectory, the high walls of which were covered in column upon column of names in black, gently slanting, as if a steady breeze were ruffling through the letters. Nobody in the room was paying the slightest attention to these names, though on the wall above our table I noticed the line *C.M.P. Standish 1904–1909. Wic.Coll.*; all the names above him had been underlined thinly in red. I wanted to point this out to my new neighbour, but held back, fearing to draw down attention upon myself.

For breakfast there were kippers with soggy fried bread and stewed tomatoes. The master at the head of the table told us we had to eat everything, and not to leave a scrap on our plates.

'But, sir . . . why do we have to eat it all?' asked Palgrave brightly.

'Because if you don't it's a waste,' the master replied.

'But, sir . . . why is it a waste?'

'Because people unluckier than you have to live on less,' the master said, a little more sternly this time.

'But, sir, we could . . .' *Sir. Sir* . . . but this was no knight with a jousting beam.

'Shut IT, boy,' bellowed the master, as yet unhoarse. 'I'll wait all day if I have to,' he continued, invoking that tired threat common to all schoolmasters to which we would all soon be so accustomed that the very sound of it, like the grumpy refrain of an elderly relative, would become almost reassuring. Though that first morning its minatory charge was still fresh and fearsome, and everybody dutifully began scraping their plates until the bone albedo reflected back the shop-floor-watted bulbs high above our heads, while I sat there trying not to look at the one food I detest most in the world, this Portuguese man-of-war beached on my plate, the very presence of which had already collaterally prejudiced the matter of the sullen kipper and sodden fried bread which I might otherwise have ventured. Solemnly I remembered my dunes of smooth *there is no smoother* Skippy, my Grape Nuts *that stay crunchy in milk*, like stepping over pebbles in shallow water, the smaller ones catching for a moment between the toes, the larger pleasantly gritty and sharp, printing themselves into the gums, and I wondered whether I would ever again look

15

down into the white morning through the slats of the veranda blinds while below out of the sunlight Omer shammied down the Plymouth under the carob trees. And only when the master's attention was distracted momentarily by some hooting on an adjacent table was I able to flick the thing away and under, though for weeks afterwards I would draw in my chair with cringing caution for fear of what lay beneath. In time I would manage to have myself excused from stewed tomatoes on religious grounds. I was able to convince the master that I belonged to that particular sect of the Eastern Church which held that Eve had tempted Adam with a tomato. The master took it all very seriously and would send boys down to the Pigs' Table, or worse, if they even so much as mentioned a tomato.

After breakfast and chapel each of the new men was committed to the care of a *pater* whose task it was to be our guide during the first two weeks of term. My pater was a wiry boy called Ferrers, hardly taller than I was, with a pensive face and long dark eyelashes. At first I thought there was something peculiar about his nose until I realised that this was because it resembled my own. His tweed jacket was streaked with ink stains, and had leather patches down the arms, and a leather strip beside the buttonholes along the front. This battle-hardened look impressed me. By the first break, however, when we queued outside a hatch from the kitchens for Peak Freans and weak orange cordial, it had already become evident from the peevish looks with which he greeted the other boys that Ferrers was embarrassed by my presence and resented having to be a pater, so I thought it better to relieve him of his duties and set off to explore on my own.

I had never seen such long corridors, not even half as long as these. The corridor on the ground floor ran the whole length of the school, from the gym at one end, to the headmaster's study at the other. Down towards the gym life shrank away into nothing, like something spied down the wrong end of a telescope. I had only gone about a third of the way along when a master in a duffel-coat suddenly shot out from nowhere. He circled me slowly, at his leisure, examining me from various angles, as if he were checking for cracks. 'You shouldn't be here on your own. Who's your pater?' His breath held the scent of the tideless rock pools below the corniche where I would hunt for scuttle crabs among the gull droppings and slippery algae. He took out a pocket book and slapped the pages backwards and forwards, giving it a good dusting, until he found what he wanted. 'Ah, Ferrers . . . when you see him tell him to report back to me. Mr Cleeve.' Then he stretched out his long arm and shook me gently by the hand.

That night the boy with the bushy red hair who was called Sackville dispatched Standish to a position halfway down the stone stairs. He was not to move until he was relieved. If he saw raiders coming he had to give a sharp whistle, and if he saw a master he had to give a double whistle. That morning Ferrers had described with some relish how the look-out was usually considered *expendable* due to the fact that immediately he had raised the alarm *water-defences* would be activated around the door to the dormitory which meant that he would have to choose between a *full wetting* and facing the enemy from an *exposed vanguard salient*. But since the morning break Ferrers had remained aloof and refused to answer any more of my questions, and that night in the dormitory he was careful to look away when he passed the end of my bed.

Earlier in the evening I had watched with some interest as a fight had developed between Ferrers and a burly older boy called Stobart whom Ferrers had caught in the act of trying to make off with one of his wooden-knobbed drawers of which Stobart claimed prior ownership. Ferrers had deftly pinned the larger boy down in a tight neck-hold while he kicked out wildly like a trapped wildebeest. All the other seniors had surrounded the pair in a close circle and stamped their feet, chanting *Ferr-Et Ferr-Et* louder and louder until finally the other boy squealed out *I submit* and Ferrers released him. While the fight had been in progress Palgrave had stepped into the circle and gamely chanted with the rest, but when the group had broken up Sackville and a couple of others rounded on him for being an *impudent worm* and kicked him back to his bed where he was left blubbing. Meanwhile the contested drawer had disappeared, and despite a thorough search Ferrers had been unable to recover it.

After lights-out Standish returned shivering to his bed. When he had sent Palgrave to relieve him, Sackville sat up on his chest and addressed the dormitory, 'Tonight all the seniors and the new men introduce themselves, as at the beginning of every new year.' Someone sniggered a couple of beds down. Sackville threw a hairbrush at him, and continued, 'We each say what our name is and what our fathers do, and if there's liars they get the stocks.' He paused again, waiting to see if there was anyone bold enough to interrupt.

'My name's Sackville Patrol Leader. And my father visits farmers.'

'Ferrers . . . My father goes to committees.' There was a perfunctory chorus of *Ferr-Et Ferr-Et*.

'I'm called Barnsley. My father drives a Massive Ferguson.'

Another short chorus of braying followed, after which, in an enclitic falsetto, Stobart announced himself. 'Myname's-Stobart father'sbank.'

This occasioned a rather longer chorus, led by Ferrers:

18

'Stubby turd. Stubby DONG. Tubby PISSER.'

'NO SMOKING IN THIS COMPARTMENT. Stub it out. STUB HIM OUT.'

Sackville let this go on only so long before calling the assembly to order by throwing another hairbrush in the direction of Ferrers, after which the remaining two boys, Savage and Sackville Minor, both of whose fathers also visited farmers, introduced themselves without much further incident. It was now the turn of the new men on the other side, and after a little coaxing, the boy on the end of the row with the one-eyed bear was persuaded to speak.

'My father . . . goes up to London. My name is Cooke.' There was immediate uproar.

'Cook. COOK. Haahaaahaaa.'

'What? Like someone who works in the kitchens?'

'Like a prole, you mean.'

'Like a scully.'

'A pantry monkey.'

'You mean a SPONGER. A gutter grub.'

'SCRUBBER, SCRUBBER, SLAVE, SLAVE.'

And so on until finally Sackville tired of it and called them to heel. After some hesitation the next boy spoke up.

'My name's de Lacey and my pa's retired.' Again there was mayhem.

'Durr Lacy was it?'

'What like DURRRR LACY.' Boys were stretching their cheeks and patting them, making a hollow clock-clock sound.

'I forgot my brain. DURRRR. *Clock-Clock.* DUURRRR.'

'Lacy. Isn't that what girls wear?' pondered Ferrers, and the others took up this theme.

'You're really a girl not a boy. Lacy *GIRLY*. GIRL. GIRL.'

When the chorus had become a little too monotonous for his taste Sackville concluded, 'From now on you answer to

19

GIRL and nothing else.' (Cooke would be joining the ranks of those unfortunates like Hogg, Bush, and the French boy called Ponge, who were expected to answer to their own names.)

Next it was the turn of the boy with the badger. In a tremulous, halting voice he announced, 'I'm Jeremy and my father's called First Secretary.'

Immediately the balling and hooting started up again, accompanied this time by a full percussion section with toothbrushes and combs beating on the plastic mugs and the tops of the wooden chests. Barnsley was down on the floor thumping on an empty trunk. Savage had got up on his bed and was banging a tea-tray with the heel of his Sunday brogue. Above the tumult could be heard: 'Only POOFters use first names. Poofter. GERM, POOFTER-WORM.' (Some twenty years later these same boys would be introducing themselves in mixed company, 'First names only, please,' under strip-lights in a church basement off the Fulham Road, but that's a different story.)

Standish's *piano* introduction was submerged in the roar, and I hoped this would be my fate also, but as I began speaking there was an abrupt silence. *My father is a dean in the Middle East.* The reaction was a little slow at first.

'Does that mean you're a foreigner?'

'Is that in Yankland?'

'Is that like James Dean?'

'Son of a Gun. HOWDY PARDNER.'

Then some bright spark suggested that the Middle East was where Jews came from. This brought up a good response.

'JEW. JEW. Jewboy. Jewnose.' As they warmed to the theme they began pulling Pinocchio gestures from their noses.

'Jews Jew people, don't they? Jew NOSE. JEWDONG.'

20

It seemed you didn't need a bad name for Jew, like being called Cooke. But then, just as the Jew chant was becoming a little played out, Ferrers helpfully suggested that the Middle East was also where Arabs came from, and all hell broke loose.

'Does your father ride a CAMEL? How many wives does he have?'

'Is he the colour of crap? Does he live in a tent?'

'Do you wipe your bottom with your hand?'

'Hey, Ayrab, where's the tea-towel? Where's your dagger?'

'STAB HIM. STAB HIM.'

I thought at least if I told them my name it might be over quicker, but this only provided more material to work on. They chewed over the name in triumph, exulting in the stubborn foreignness of its syllables. *Shadrach ShaRR DraCCHH.*

'What sort of a name's that. SHAY-DRAK. Isn't that a coon name?'

'Isn't that a WOG name?'

'Hey. Banana Boy. Egg-Nog. MINSTREL. Jungle Bunny. Blubber Face.'

'OOOH NUTZULHAZULNUTS. Cover 'dem in CHOCOLATE.'

The charivari was building up to a crescendo now, and Ferrers was in full song. *SHHitter. SHHtupper. SHHnauser. Shpuker. SHHCRAPPER.*

I realized too late that I had spoken back, the whine of drumming and name-calling dying away like a sudden drop in air pressure. Even as I spoke I cursed my invisible ventriloquist. 'Don't you know that we went to church and had baths when you were still throwing each other into bogs?'

'Into BOGS?'

'Yes. Yes. Into bogs . . . and when you were painting yourselves blue with mud we had already calculated the

21

distance to the moon.' There was a momentary silence, a short intake of breath, then the Devil's Kitchen again.

'Who wants to go to chapel?' Sackville enquired mincingly.

'Only a JESUS CREEPER.'

'Only a GODSOC.'

'A JESUSCOON asking to get SOCKED.'

Projectiles were coming over in some number now. Shampoo bottles, conkers, soap, hair-brushes, toothpaste. I was beginning to recognize their different reports as they slammed into the wall above; some would crack open and dribble down into my hair. Once the bunging got seriously underway all the other noises fell off. There was someone lobbing over whole drawers. Germ and Girl had taken shelter under their beds. Standish was throwing back what he could. I came forward and crouched behind one of the drawers that had fallen at the foot of the bed. Conkers buzzed down making the wood resonate into my fingers. When the torches came on I abandoned the drawer and retreated under the bed.

Something bright had spluttered across the room and come down at the foot of Standish's bed, then another, landing higher up by the window. There was the sweet scent and fizzle of singeing: the same scent that Omer carried back in his sage-green chauffeur's cap with the whiff of plots and pomatum from the barbers on rue Abdul-Aziz. Above, on the window-ledge, a glorious burning bush of a sparkler danced and hissed. The firing had died away. Everybody had stopped to watch the fountains of light. Then the shrill alarm sounded and all the seniors put on their dressing-gowns and made for the door. Down the chilly stone steps and the endless corridors I followed the tide of boys out on to the front drive where the whole school was assembling, standing at ease by patrol on the damp gravel. We waited until our

22

name was called by the master taking Fire Practice, and then struggled to find the way back to our uncertain beds, groping down the unlit passages with their smell of carbolic and stale cabbage which we would soon cease to notice for ever.

blood feud

The school buildings stood on that ridge of hills known as Oliver's Battery high above the western face of the town, the prospect of which was partially obscured by the dense strips of beeches and horse-chestnuts bordering the front drive which were marked Out of Bounds. It was from the vantage of these hills that the Lord Protector had chosen to cannonade the ancient town below which could occasionally be glimpsed through the thin aerosol of mist rising up from the water-meadows to the south. Up until the last century these meadows had been flooded in the winter months through a series of channels and sluices to provide the richest pasture for the Easter lambs; now they were the province of amphibious trippers and school botany classes. We had been told that the town itself had once been the capital of all Christian England, the seat of legendary warrior kings, but all I had seen was a muggy high street and some boys outside the Wimpy with long hair and silly lapels, smoking in the drizzle.

The immediate world beyond the school and Hobson Wood was spectral, discontinuous, glimpsed through condensation, from a taxi or a passing train. Glimpsed yet unapprehended, this world was possessed of a sublime irrelevance; the smoke from the tower of the town hospital, visitors to the garden centre next door, the comings and goings around the bus stop on the Sarum Road: we observed such things with the glacial indifference of Bedou tribesmen watching a 747 slowly passing across their empty horizon.

If you looked up from the bottom of the rimy fields, the school building with its massed central tower, strutted flag masts and looming shoulders resembled a giant Dreadnought, something once awesome, but now earth-bound, washed-up. This is how the pictures tell us the Ark ponderously appeared, high-and-dry on Ararat. But as you close in the monumental image dissolves. The buildings have that charred and pock-marked complexion common to northern variety theatres and station hotels. Along the front and wings wide lozenges of Hampshire flint have been set into the pumice brickwork which is stained by thick trails of pigeon droppings and the mucus overflow of the drains. Finding the porous bricks an unsuitable medium for graffiti, generations of boys had bored networks of holes and sockets into the walls which served as deposits for secret messages and as snug silos for fat petards, trophies from the annual French exchange to Versailles. Occasionally, like a shepherd stumbling upon ancient scrolls, some boy would turn up a faded old note in a long-forgotten code which had survived against the odds, lodged in one of the less frequented segments of the wall. These antique notes would be ritually dispatched (it was considered ill luck to keep them) by placing the scroll of paper upright on a flat stone and lighting the top so that the wind lifted the paper flaming into the night; not dissimilar in effect to the trick with the Amaretti wrapper.

It may have been certain peculiarities in the design of the school which had led originally to those rumours going the rounds about the buildings having served for a time as a hospital for the insane. This myth had been adapted to support many of the old school superstitions which were retold on stormy nights to intimidate the credulous. In fact I believe the place was originally built as a school and had never seen any other use with the sole exception, of course, of that four-and-a-half year period when the buildings were requisitioned by the War Ministry.

It was under this crumbling façade of pitted brick and chipped flint that the school would assemble before crossing the Sarum Road to descend into Hobson Wood. I would watch them crossing in patrols, three-across, from behind one of the high windows of the dormitory where I had been told to rest in the afternoons by the Sister who smelt pleasantly of iodine and Golden Syrup. Later I would find Palgrave and Standish in the changing rooms, pale as death and panting like old dogs, their buff denim boiler-suits (worn for all *outward activities*) coated in a thin layer of white dust. When I tried to press them about what had happened in the woods they were reluctant to answer, though Palgrave would mutter something confused about *salt-mines* and a senior called *Duff-Revel*. At that point Barnsley and the others would shamble in and the opportunity was lost to question them further. As Savage and Ferrers and Barnsley bustled into the showers they all chanted:

> *Standish wet fish,*
> *Put him in a soap dish,*
> *Chuck him down the stairs,*
> *Standish wet fish.*

But Standish did not seem to hear them as he sat on the hot-water pipes, blowing into his cupped hands, the colour

29

slowly flushing back into his cheeks like a paper bloom unfolding in still water.

When the class lists were read out some of the masters were curious to know where I came from *with a name like that*. But when I told them most said they had never heard of the place, which surprised me because it was such a large city. I felt somewhat consoled, however, when Musson, our sallow history master, casually revealed that he had served there during the war with the Australian Light Armour *mopping up the Vichy drips*. Perhaps the most peculiar reaction was that of the geography master, old Major Moss in his cherry brogues and cavalry twill the colour of boiled chard. When I told him where I came from his face suddenly lit up and he immediately asked if it was the case, as he presumed it must be, that I already *enjoyed that most precious faculty of an ear nurtured on the swelling sublimities of the Oper*, and while I fingered my ear apprehensively and tried to look as if I understood he gave me a complicit smile and instructed me to name all the principal cities in Bavaria for the benefit of the class. Known as Magyar for reasons that remained obscure, the old Major, normally one of the more mild-mannered and temperate of the masters, would suddenly fire up into a towering lather whenever he heard his name, whose origins would remain the secret of previous generations, being so much as whispered. It seemed unlikely that the Major was descended from Ural-Altaic stock, nor could he be attributed with more than a passing interest in matters Austro-Hungarian. These names we inherited owned an unyielding strangeness at their heart which we would never fully tame. Like the foreground figures in a *vedute* we lived among the ancient ruins of a race whose ways had long been forgotten.

In the break after that first geography lesson Ferrers, Savage, and two other boys I didn't recognize, were waiting for me at the end of the Peak Frean line. I felt honoured to be received by such a delegation. 'Hey, Shady, we've got something to show you.' Ferrers looked away and kept his hand up to his mouth as he spoke. I followed them through that sprawling *favela* of bog-houses and prefabs which had grown up between the back of the school and the edge of the games fields. There was a sort of Venetian complexity about the place. A maze of little alleys and yards connected long-abandoned bog-houses with corrugated-iron sheds and black creosoted huts left behind by the army. The tutelary spirit of this derelict space was Johnny Bunts, an odd-job man with greasy rat tails and indigo tattoos who possessed a Magwitch-like faculty for appearing suddenly from behind walls waving something from his tool box. If you saw Johnny it was best to run for it, so I had been told. Nobody had ever got close enough to make out the subject of his tattoos, though there was much speculation on this topic.

As we penetrated deeper into the maze the going became darker. We could no longer hear the sounds of ragging from the corridors. After crossing a small mossy yard and passing down a narrow alley with wire netting above it, a trap for old gym shoes, biscuit tins and games socks, Ferrers led the way into an abandoned bog-house, the walls of which were covered in eau-de-Nil tiles beaded with condensation. Ferrers had opened the door to one of the cubicles down at the bottom and was pointing excitedly at something inside. The others pushed ahead into the cubicle. I was afraid I might not get a proper look at whatever it was so I pushed in after them. But as I went forward I felt something pressing on my ankles: suddenly my legs lifted from under me, and as the world turned upside-down I caught a glimpse of my Parker 51s scuttling away under the partition. For some moments I hung there, a dummy, a *dangling man*, the tip of my father's uncreasable silk tie drifting forlornly into

31

the bowl beneath me. The prettiest thing down there was the limescale, crawling out over the china like lichen over a garden statue.

Who's being chucked into the bog now, Shady? This they repeated until it grew into a rhythmical chant, becoming gradually more amplified so that even if I had thought of something to appease them it would not have been heard. When the chanting halted there was only one voice, one I did not recognize. *This isn't for being a Wopo by the way. This is for sneaking on Ferret.* I was being winched slowly downwards, a sweet dead smell rising into my flaring nostrils. The scent was weaving its lazy way down my throat, teasing my stomach walls into spasms. And then suddenly the remains of the morning's kipper and fried bread sprayed out over someone's grey-flannel crotch, and as the boy staggered backwards I sensed the grasp on one of my ankles slackening. I kicked out with all my strength, feeling the satisfying reports up my leg as the Clarke's Commando hit home. A pair of glasses shot off behind the cistern. As I landed crouching on the damp floor Savage was backing away, clutching his dirty hanky to his nose. 'Pax,' he said crossing his digit fingers in front of him, 'Pax.' I shut my eyes and kept kicking until there was nothing left to kick. And when I opened my eyes my foot had gone all numb and I was alone, and for a while I could make out nothing in the shadows between the cubicles, and when I closed my eyes again I saw only the flickering remains of my first summer in England, the dying light through the tall casement windows, the cowardly flies, the shocking greenness of it all, and my English grandmother walking down through the paddock in her wellingtons to check on the campers, calling through the Yorkshire dusk after her lame old mare, 'Don't kick them, Sally dear. Remember only donkeys kick.'

Every night rumours of raids circulated through the dormitory, but after a week without incident I began to wonder if the threat of these raids might not merely be a pretext for Sackville to impose an ever more draconian discipline upon the dormitory. (The other two dormitories in the main school building, West and North, were occupied by two rival houses, the Stags and the Curlews, with the Buffaloes down in Hobson Lodge; there was little unguarded movement between the different sectors of the building after vespers when each house imposed a curfew on its surrounding corridors and washrooms.) Over the course of the week our defences had been systematically elaborated and deepened. Look-out shifts had been extended into the early hours of the morning. The first line of defence, the water trap, which had initially been composed of only a few plastic mugs on top of the door, now involved whole biscuit tins and sponge-bags brimming with water, and an extensive battery of water-bombs which had to be re-supplied every night, and an ancient conical fire extinguisher, like a giant cream dispenser. For the second line of defence, known as the *bunging line*, an arsenal comprising anything chuckable such as shoes, conkers, soap, hairbrushes, and shampoo bottles was marshalled behind bunkers constructed from upturned beds. It was anticipated that the enemy would be so concussed and demoralized from the effects of this second barrage that this would be the optimum moment for an *operational unit*, lightly armed with sock-balls and snake belts, to sortie out from behind the upturned beds with the objective of securing a hostage, preferably of senior rank. Nightly raid drills had been instituted by Sackville in which some poor saps were obliged to play the role of the enemy.

I began to look forward to my shifts as a look-out. This was the only time when one could escape the martial frenzy that had gripped the dormitory. Ever since I had been picked by Cleeve to play Theseus's mother in the school play

Ferrers and the others had been leaving me alone. They simply couldn't top this humiliation. It was one of only three female parts in the entire school repertory. Performed in strict rotation, with the same props and costumes each year, this repertory included Cleeve's own adaptations of *Galloping Foxley* and *Lord of the Flies*, along with truncated versions of *Journey's End* and *The Monkey's Paw*. For a work to be included in the school canon it was desirable that it should not include female parts, and preferably have none at all. (*The Tempest* and *Midsummer Night's Dream*, performed on alternate summers in the coomb of Hobson Wood, were the exceptions to this rule, but the uniform weirdness of the costumes, along with the fact that we had been assured that there were no actresses in Shakespeare's day, resulted in those playing female roles rarely being persecuted.)

During the first rehearsal in Milton Hall under chapel I was to address my five lines from the balcony dressed in a satin toga to Theseus below, played by Barnsley, who as I spoke was struggling to lift a papier mâché rock:

Lo! My son, first born of Aegeus,
Light of Attica, blessed of Artemis,
When you have strength sufficient,
To raise the stone in yon boscage,
The hero's sword and sandals are your own.

As Cleeve stood behind me attempting to supervise my elocutionary respiration my lungs had become filled with his brackish breath, dry and itchy as the tired air on the third and final day of a khamsin when the shop windows and parked cars along Ain Mreisse are covered in fiery slogans and love poems. While I spluttered and coughed we had proceeded to the next scene where Theseus sets forth on his raft (inherited from previous productions) with one black sail and one white, which was constructed from silver birch

34

trunks from the woods, mounted on rollers, and pulled along by some juniors attired as waves. After dispensing with the Minotaur he had given a quick ride to Ariadne, played by the sexagenarian piano mistress Mrs Postgate, and then abandoned her on the billiard table which had been converted into the island of Naxos.

I lay awake after returning from my shift, straining to catch again that dull pounding from deep inside the building. Slowly I drifted into a shallow, colourless sleep. I was awakened by a creaking noise from the window above Palgrave's bed, and then the sound of iron springs squeaking as something heavy hit his bed. In the darkness I thought I could make out a large body drop down from the fire escape on to the bed, and then crawl away along the floor. When the lights went on there were strangers everywhere. By a single bold saltus our guests had rendered Sackville's elaborate defences as irrelevant as a washing line.

Sackville and the others in his row didn't even have time to sit up in their beds. They were surrounded and clubbed down where they lay. When some finally managed to struggle out from under the blows they found themselves being bombarded with their own arsenal of shoes and conkers and hairbrushes which the visitors had immediately located. They crawled about in every direction like bewildered ants, not knowing where to turn for shelter, and while they blundered about exposed to a pummelling from every angle, their beds were being dealt a full wetting with the water-bombs, followed by a full lamp-posting. The intruders had rightly calculated that the juniors would be too entranced by the spectacle of their elders being crushed to attempt to interfere. We watched silently as the visitors set about sacking each coveted chest and despoiling its contents. All clothes and bedding were farded with shampoo and toothpaste, all books and games hurled from the open window. It was now clear why Sackville had wished to build such elaborate defences.

35

Next to the exotic majesty of these wild Scythians, Sackville and his sidekicks had been shown up as nothing more than small-time martinets. And one fighter towered above the rest, gliding across the surface of the dormitory with the grace and suppleness of a natural covering his court. His judgement of the relative distance and speed of his targets never once faltered. There was an elegant economy of power in the execution of his strokes: the blows fell sweet and sure, without a trace of overhit or wrist, his entire body working in perfect torsional balance. While his fellow fighters mostly favoured sock-balls, stuffed with hairbrushes and conkers to add punch, he preferred to use a towel, a thick knot at the end, dipped in water to harden it. This weapon he spun fast above his head like a propellor before bringing it down to test the elasticity of his opponent's stomach. While his victim, Sackville in this instance, was doubled up on the floor, winded and gasping for mercy, this dancing executioner delivered a textbook topspin overhead to the back of his neck and then danced on leaving him reeling to a further clubbing from his comrades, and as his blows connected, ribbons of water flew out, blessing our foreheads.

Ferrers was the only one in Sackville's row to escape the rout. When the attack began he had managed to scramble up and conceal himself on the wide window-ledge. I saw his whey face peeping out from behind the thin cloth as our neighbours finally pulled out, taking with them three hostages locked in half-Nelsons, and a procession of trophy drawers piled high with conkers, sparklers, catapults and sheath knives. Motionless we listened to the dull drumming of their sock-balls on the wooden panelling as they headed away down the long first-floor corridor. On their way out they had sent Palgrave back; he had been too frightened to return before being relieved.

And when I woke in the early morning, I saw three

figures, shuffling back through the iron light to their beds, choking back their blubbing.

'Guess who was given six hard ones by the headman before Vespers?' It was the first time Ferrers had spoken to me since the incident in the bog-house. Two nights had passed since the raid and Sackville had ordered lights-out early again. Some boys were reading by torchlight under their rugs. There was a faint glow above the beds of the readers.

'Who?'

'Duff-Revel.'

'So?'

'So someone told him you were the one who sneaked on him for going out on the fire escape.'

'But that's a lie.'

'Better watch yourself in the woods, Shady.'

live and let die

It did not take long to discover that team sports were not especially popular at North Hill. When sides from Horace Downs and the Griffin School were visiting, a gang of juniors would have to be dragooned into supporting the home team. After the match the visitors were customarily given a pelting with dried mud in the changing rooms; there would be more trouble at tea if the visitors failed to surrender their Penguins to the gallant losers. The only sports approached competitively were athletics and tennis, and these were pursued with such fanatical devotion that even the masters in charge complained at parades about the *blight of unsporting behaviour*. In team sports, however, slackness and malingering were the accepted way. Sister Gab's surgery was routinely full of boys with unusual complaints; recondite symptoms were imitated with the help of *Black's Medical Dictionary* of which Barnsley owned a copy. The games lists were a palimpsest of revisions and forgeries. After one small boy, caught in the act of trying to delete his name, had explained that he was *just testing* his 51, there had been a general crack-down on shirkers, but this initiative had petered out after only a few weeks.

Snow or hail was no deterrent to the playing of rugger or football. The bitter cold on those exposed fields was only exacerbated by the frequent interruptions on account of conspicuous fouling, cod injuries, histrionic diving, and the ball being deliberately kicked deep into touch. What the score was when the game was finally over no one knew or cared. By far the most active person on the pitch was Fisher the ref who weaved about over the frozen mud blowing his cracked whistle in a giant pair of navy-blue shorts. Like the man in the slimming ad above the bus stop on the Sarum Road he was entirely dwarfed by his own clothes.

Olim renato nomine magister vostrum Ieremias Piscator. We all knew by heart the first line from Fisher's celebrated translation of Beatrix Potter, though he was far too diffident to impose the text upon us as mandatory reading. It was difficult to tell when he was blushing because his face had been scraped meat-raw by blunt shaving. In class Fisher always wore an ash-grey short-sleeved pullover, wiry, like horse bristle. He was so hirsute, I used to wonder sometimes if it had not been woven from his own hair. From a distance he looked as if he'd been up to his elbows in a coal bunker.

Fisher patiently taught us the myths by handing out unseens illustrated with primitive line drawings of his own making, without relief or shading, blueprints for the ancient figures carved into the chalk escarpments of the surrounding countryside. *Saturn devours his children. Pallas springs fully armed from the head of Jupiter. Cadmus sowing the dragon's teeth at Thebes* . . . the warriors shooting up out of the ground, pitching into each other with sword and spear, and in the background the smoking city the strongest will rebuild. This rebarbative myth was executed in the same delinquent scrawl as the so-called *wartime cartoons* on the sides of the black creosoted sheds, which, despite the frequent overpaintings of Johnny Bunts, kept emerging again *penti-*

mento like those X-rayed eidolons which skulk behind famous oil paintings. (Sometimes through the slatted bog-house windows after lights-out I would glimpse a huddled figure in a duffel-coat down among the sheds. Something thin and glinting in his hands. Dividers perhaps, or a compass. As stealthily as a hitman opens his cushioned attaché case – this was how they eased the lids off their geometry tins; of course the Jackal was the great school hero.) Fisher walked with a slight stoop which was grotesquely imitated by certain wags who followed him down the corridors. When he saw their reflections in the window panes he would abruptly pivot on his own axis and give them a quick cuffing with the back of his hand. Fisher was perhaps the kindest of the masters.

It did not take long to understand that there were essentially four modes of baiting, or *brocking*, as it was sometimes known.[1] These comprised *Face*, *Call*, *Walk* and *Gesture*. This variety allowed for flexibility in different environments. For example, if one was in the dark, or in a closed bog cubicle, anything other than the *Call* would have been redundant. However, if a master was present in a classroom, one might wish to confine oneself to discreet *Faces* and *Gestures*. Over a long distance, from one end of a pitch to another, only the *Walk* might effectively communicate the intended message. Wherever possible brockers combined all four modes in an integrated performance. For instance, a boy with a reputation for a lack of co-ordination, or physical ineptitude, such as Stobart, would find himself represented in the figure of the *malco* which shuffled along with bowed head, Frankenstein-like, and was characterized by a gaping mouth, hanging jaw, Neanderthal grunts, and frequent head scratching.

[1] This word is possibly derived from the old country term for badger-baiting; the *OED* has OE *broc(f)* from OBrit *brokkos*: a badger.

43

One apparent drawback of the brocking system was that the vast majority of standard brocks related to foreigners or regional types of which there were few living specimens within the school. Thus any boy with a tincture of regional associations, or foreign characteristics, such as curly hair or a greasy complexion, was identified with a foreign place or people and brocked accordingly. This practice led to certain curious anomalies. A boy called Somerset, though he lived in London, would be baited as a West Country yokel. Similarly a boy such as Douglas with curly black hair and full lips was known as Shaka and brocked for a Zulu. More curious perhaps was that the brocked themselves came to identify with those regions and peoples with which they had been compared. When there was a slide lecture on mining, for instance, and Barnsley found himself brocked from all sides as a *scully northerner*, though his family had lived in Norfolk for generations, he would rally to the miners' cause with a degree of heartfelt conviction and eloquence which would have put many union men to shame. Similarly, when he heard the Portuguese kitchen staff being addressed as *guttergrubs* or *mop monkeys*, Cooke would take this as a direct infraction of his own honour, heaping invective and blows upon the offenders. Without the Saturday-afternoon films screened in Milton many of the traditional brocks might have passed into desuetude. But here there were foreigners aplenty: Nips in *Bridge over the River Kwai*, Wopos in *The Italian Job*, Jerries in *Patten* and *Battle of the River Plate*, Jews in the Biblical epics, Ayrabs in *Lawrence of Arabia*, each hailed with their own generic calls and gestures.

After lunch on Sunday those boys who had not been taken out by their parents, or someone else's parents, gathered on the front drive for the crossing to Hobson Wood. It was the first time I had tried my new boiler-suit, and the first time I had ever worn denim; it was stiff and shiny and felt a little like greaseproof paper. We were lined up in patrols, three-across, Curlews first, then the Buffaloes, the Stags, and lastly ourselves, the Hounds. I was between Standish and Palgrave, as usual, whose faces were the same dead-white as the things that floated in jars on the top shelves of the science room. I think I tried to joke with them about this but they both turned away, fixing their gaze into the dark thickets beside the drive. As the patrols ahead of us began to move off a shudder went through their bodies the way it does through a horse about to bolt. Moss was waiting ahead of us inspecting everyone as they filed across the Sarum Road. Standing beside him was Sister Gab (if she had another name I never heard anyone use it) in her blue nurse's uniform with a pocket watch pinned to her left breast. As we came alongside she whispered something in the Major's ear and he pulled up the patrol. I could see Standish and Palgrave were staring at her with longing spaniel eyes. This was their last chance of a reprieve, but Sister Gab had already turned to go. As we passed the Major stretched out and grabbed me by the ear-lobe. 'Off to surgery and no divagations on the way, boy.' Those were his words, exactly.

Conditions were generally better in the sickbay than in the dormitory. There were fewer pigeons outside the windows in the mornings. We were allowed to wear our thick Clydella pyjamas and our dressing-gowns all through the day. There was even a radiator in the room which came on from seven until nine in the mornings, and then from five until eight at night. It made a gentle hacking noise. And there were dark lambs which circled, the shadows of a mobile, over the ribbed wallpaper.

I was sharing on the first day with a senior who was about to take his Winchester Entrance. Sister Gab had told me that I would have to remain in the sickbay until there was no longer any risk of my infecting the other boys. The molasses linctus, which I had sucked from a bent tablespoon slick as a relic kissed over the centuries, had released a sudden convulsion of restive energy that had gradually ebbed away to leave behind it a gentle, quilted melancholy. For two hours the other boy in the room ignored me completely and read his history book *The New Barbarism*, but as the light started to fade he put down the book and began to speak at length without turning to look at me. His voice was surprisingly deep, the words intoned with the solemn, resigned quaver of an evensong formulatory. It was as if he had said those same words so many times before that they had become emptied of everything except their dying music. For what could have been hours or moments I drifted half-insensibly on the slow currents of his disembodied voice, not caring where they might draw me, until the sudden darkness beyond the window, like the snap of a hypnotist's fingers, startled me back into the present. I told myself then, as I often did, that I would look back on this moment at some remote point in the future and it would all seem to have taken place a very long time ago. All that was visible now out in the November night was the white mast above the tower, a dark flag restlessly flexing. Turning to look at me for the first time the boy explained that it was a school custom to raise a red flag whenever the sickbay was occupied. Before telephones were in common use this had been the most effective means of attracting the attention of the doctor down in the town. It was just a tradition now.

The autumn nights up on that hill had their own paintbox

of darkness, luminous, variegated. As the night closed in around the hill smelling of coal fires and rotting leaves and wet bark the lights along the lower corridors and in the classrooms began to turn yellow and sickly. It seemed as if at any moment they might dicker out altogether. This darkness enclosing the school buildings shut out all sounds from the world outside like a great black muffler. Even the shaking bus on the Sarum Road had been silenced. Though earlier that evening the older boy had told me that when he first came to the school there were still those who spoke of the rattling of tin cups and plates which used to carry up the Sarum Road from the prison on the nights before a hanging.

The encroaching nights had persuaded me that I might never again see my house, hear the electric cicadas singing, walk barefoot over matted crabgrass, but I longed to explore this exotic new world of mists and darkness which was already eclipsing memories of blanching light over Mediterranean beaches and all the phantasmagoria of summer.

I had to wait in Sister Gab's surgery for the doctor to come and examine me. Earlier there had been some boys ragging up and down *shirkers' passage* but they had been seen off and everything was quiet now. I waited for the doctor with a certain foreboding. I had heard the boys in the dormitory telling strange jokes about him. Also I had lied to Sister Gab about having had my tonsils out, and when the doctor shone his special torch in my mouth he would discover them. During the night I had had a vision of my tonsils floating like lychees in a kidney bowl. The breakfast master had made the whole school wait until I got them down.

The doctor was late and there was nothing to do in the surgery. Every surface in the room, the top of the pine table, the plastic seats of the chairs, the partitions, had been coated in white emulsion which had been picked away in places by waiting boys. Apart from a National Trust calendar (open at

Ickworth) and an eye chart, the only decoration hanging on the walls was a small framed tapestry, presumably the work of Sister Gab or one of the matrons, which read:

A Scotsman: keeps the Sabbath and everything else he can get his hands on. A Welshman: prays on his knees on Sundays and on everyone else the rest of the week. An Irishman: has no principles and is prepared to die for them. An Englishman: a self-made man who worships his master.

I pondered this for a while until the doctor arrived wearing a russet waistcoat and a polka-dot bow-tie. I was almost disappointed to see how unintimidating and genial he was after all that I had heard. After listening to my chest he asked me to cough, and as I coughed he lightly fingered my testicles between his thumb and forefinger, as if he were checking plums in the market. It only lasted a moment and then I was allowed to go back to my room.

The days in the sickbay had their own soft tides and cadences. Twice every morning, and twice every afternoon except Sundays, I would hear the scraping of a spade in the coal bunker beneath my window as a Moroccan workman in a woolly tam-o'-shanter filled up his shuttle to take over to the headman's study. Sometimes he would look up and see me watching him from the window. He would give me a weary and complicit smile, and I would wave back. Soon I began to feel guilty if I did not go to the window when I heard the scraping.

After the bell sounded for the first break there would be absolute silence for a minute or more, more absolute than the silence that had preceded that minute. Then I would hear the first muffled screeches as boys began scrumming for places outside the Peak Frean hatch down at the kitchens. Every break I went to the window and watched the flight of balsa-wood gliders from the balcony of the First XI pavilion.

On days with a steady eastern breeze those with wide wingspans rose effortlessly into the bright autumn air; for a while it would seem that they were going to soar away through the horse-chestnuts and disappear down the hill, but in the end they usually landed with a graceful slither in the rank grass beyond the muddy pitches. Many of the smaller gliders were quickly caught up in spiralling eddies or were buffeted by a sudden oncoming blast and plunged nose-down into the concrete of the pavilion steps. Occasionally I saw a senior wander out from under the pavilion and trample on one of the fallen gliders.

On days when it was raining the gliders were not launched and I would watch the juniors pushing each other down the grass banks at the top of which there was a row of great spreading chestnut trees. Sometimes they would play at being shot. One of the boys on top of the bank would call down *Shoot me shoot me* and someone below would oblige with a stick in the shape of a Sten or a Mauser. The victim would clutch his stomach (always his stomach) and totter about at the top of the bank before abandoning himself to the fall, groaning and gasping as he rolled downwards to play out his final death throes at the bottom of the bank for as long as they could be histrionically sustained. It was apparent in these games, choreographed from the Saturday war films, that there were always at a single time rather more being shot than actually firing. It was not uncommon in the absence of shooters for the same boy to loose off a fusillade in one place, then stop time and run around to take up his position in the line of fire and begin his dying fall, only to rise from the ground fighting again moments later like one of the legendary warriors of Thebes.

At about nine every evening Sister Gab came in to watch me say my prayers before she switched out the lights. If I took too long she began tapping on the wainscot with her walking shoes. On Saturdays and Sundays she brought in honeyed milk and Clubs and a napkin which she tucked into my pyjamas, to catch the crumbs, she said. Once it was dark outside I watched the pale lozenges of light under the eaves of St Cross and North, though there was little to see except the weak light itself from behind which came faint cries and falderals in voices I did not yet recognize.

Twice a week, for the duration of my evening prayers, I allowed myself to think of home, no more or I might never return. *It is always the same. I am in the front of the Plymouth on the bench seat beside Omer. It is dark but the streets are still humid. We are driving down through the aquarium of rue Hamra. On either side the alleys are strung with torn bunting and festoons of wedding lights that shine dimly like the spangled plastic necklaces which the girls from the camps holding their babies wrapped in keffieh offer outside the pavement cafés along Abdul-Aziz; I've never actually seen them make a sale. The street ahead is blocked by an old Sudanese in a scarlet tarboush pushing a heaped wheelbarrow. Omer doesn't bother to hoot. He knows he won't be heard. Even with the windows closed and the air-conditioning full on the smell of cinnamon and roasting peanuts fills the car, overpowering the scent of Omer's cedarwood worry beads. We are on our way back from our first Bond film, a matinée at L'Étoile. Her mouth stained clown-red from sucking on pome-granates, my American companion Emmy Lindbergh is sulking in the back, chewing on the plastic figures which sprout from the periscope-tower of her submarine. Despite the deep-sea tinted glass the elegant ladies of Hamra can see how white the sun has turned her hair. They shake their scarabed fingers and call out endear-ments — Ya Habibti — Chou-Chou — Poupon — but she ignores them. For a moment I think I see my mother coming out from one of the doorways between the boutiques across the road. As we pull away her figure is lost behind the high fins of the oncoming traffic. But it couldn't have been her because when we reach home she is there waiting on the veranda dressed as a Japanese Empress in a long brocaded kimono and curling fingernails and a black lacquered wig with what look like spillikins sticking out of the back. She fishes a few pebbles of ice from her cocktail and dabs my eyes and my nose, and then she dabs around Emmy's mouth until the ice slips away on to the floor.*

my enemy's enemy

When we had crossed the Sarum Road we followed the narrow, overgrown lane down to Hobson Lodge. On the way through the silver-birch woods boys would pluck switches from the hedgerows and knock down the lobes of pale fungus which grew over the birch barks and then mash them into pieces on the shale drive. Heads lowered, crunching the loose shale under their wellingtons, ignoring the lumps of fungus being flicked at them, the juniors trudged on still in formation, while Duff-Revel and his chosen fighters lagged behind so they could reach their secret dry caches in the thickets where they stowed their sapling wands and pointed staves. I had tried repeatedly to imitate this practice by bagging choice weapons in polythene and hiding them under rocks and in the dense thickets at the head of the drive, but I was never once able to find them again the following week. Though I retraced my steps with care to what I was certain had been the same bush or rock where I had left them I found they were always gone. Then some weeks later I would begin to imagine I had seen Duff-Revel or Douglas casually wielding one of my whittled ashplants, yet I knew this was impossible because I had checked from one of the tallest spying firs that Duff-Revel and the other fighters were still occupied down at the camp before I had concealed my weapons.

As the terms passed I had become more familiar with the topography of the woods. Gradually I had grown more confident of escaping capture and slavery in the chalk mines. Some wets like Savage and Stobart would attempt to seek sanctuary with the master but it was only a matter of time before he retired into the lodge to smoke his pipe and they were immediately herded off and put to work tunnelling in one of the darkest corners of the pits. Others such as Girl and Bass would endeavour to buy their freedom by offering tribute in the form of sheath knives and bird catapults. This was a risky stratagem however for there was no guarantee that the fighters would keep their side of the bargain. More often than not the tribute would be seized by the fighters as contraband and those who had tried to buy their freedom would be dealt a full wanding and led off blubbing to the mines. The sapling wands bit keenly, even through the thick denim of the boiler-suits, and continued to burn through the afternoon, leaving behind a sequence of tidy laddered weals which were called *trademarks*.

Most boys had chosen to submit voluntarily to slavery in the mines, hoping in time to earn their manumission and promotion through the ranks of the camp hierarchy from *sapper* up to *messenger*, and eventually initiation into the fighting order itself; like the Marmelukes, Duff-Revel and his fighters had all begun their distinguished careers as slaves. Due to the school's tenuous historical connections with Baden-Powell, whose portrait hung in the corridor opposite the headman's study, afternoons in Hobson Wood were officially intended to provide the opportunity for standard scouting pursuits such as building fires, cooking chipolatas, and distinguishing *cirrus* from *cumulus*, but these activities only served as an effective cover for the diffuse structure of the camp around the chalk pits which had been excavated by generations of boys into a warren of fox-holes and interconnected passages. Any boys who tried to escape the camp were known as *quarry* and they would be hunted down by roving units of fighters. Those who were captured were given public wandings or nettlings and pushed down the muddy banks beside the lodge before they were put to work in the pits. Any quarry who were known to be claustrophobic were treated to a live burial in the mounds of rotting leaves at the base of the banks, or sealed in a fox-hole and left to dig themselves out with their hands. These same boys, if unfortunate enough to be taken hostage during dormitory raids, were often shut up in trunks and, before they were beaten, had Gladstone bags zipped up over their heads; possibly this was why the claustrophobics were known as Liquorice-Allsorts men.

Though the denseness of the firs afforded good cover and the fallen branches convenient camouflage, the fighters were also able to take full advantage of these conditions discreetly to track the quarry and mount sudden ambushes at close quarters. To begin with I had moved around the woods with the Sackvilles and Barnsley but it soon became apparent that this group did not take sufficient care to conceal its tracks through the woods and resorted too frequently to verbal communications rather than signs and whistles. On my second outing with this group we were ambushed out at the boundary path on the southern reaches of the woods. By the time that the Sackvilles and Barnsley had discovered they were unable to swing their long staffs due to the closeness of the branches, the ambushers, armed with stumps and short pointed staves well adapted to fighting in confined spaces, had closed in and clubbed them into submission. I had only managed to escape by burying myself in some tall brambles which clawed my arms and neck and crudded my hair and face with the juice of bitter broken berries. Only Ferrers seemed to return week after week uncaptured to the lodge, slipping back apparently unnoticed among Palgrave and Standish and the others who stood about a little unsteadily coated in a fine layer of chalk dust, gaping up the drive with the same dislocated, unbelieving stare of people who have just been dragged free from the bombed rubble of what was once their office or home.

For a long time after my release from the sickbay Sister Gab had sent me to Milton on Wednesday and Sunday afternoons while the rest of the school went down to the woods. Even on bright winter days the hall was full of shadows. It was forbidden to turn on the lights. The bars of sunlight seemed to get fouled up in the lead between the panes and swallowed into the dark tarn of the panelling. In some ways I preferred the dull days. I would drift round and round that long hall, never settling anywhere for long, running my fingers over the joins in the panels, listening for the tread of a master approaching the gallery above the hall from which I had addressed Theseus and from which gliders would be launched during indoor breaks, though masters seldom came to check on me. Empty schools possess their own special type of silence, a sort of hoax, tense and unnatural, as if everyone is in hiding and will spring out at any moment. When the school was full there were many noises too shy to make themselves heard, and these would reveal themselves to me, one by one, as I explored the secret archipelagos in the dark panelling: the unseasonal buzzing of flies, the dring-dring of a typewriter, the reluctant grating of a mower out on the fields, clutches of a harpsichord concerto from somewhere in the masters' lodge.

Returning the stare of the founder whose sunken, Pre-Raphaelite eyes reproached those who sought to escape them, I would cross the hall at that narrow isthmus which was usually occupied by boys playing Risk and Dover Patrol who would huddle protectively over the boards as seniors passed, like goatherds guarding their fires against the desert wind. Towards the end of the hall, opposite the billiard table, there was a locked cabinet known as *the museum* which was never opened but occasionally served as a landing zone in glider trials. This cabinet contained a flattened python skin, a gas mask, some rare birds' eggs, prints of fractured Kouroi, and a champion pike in a glass case. High enough above the cabinet to be beyond the reach of those who climbed on top of it there hung Kitchener's sword and an illegible framed letter from Lord Roberts to the school. At the opposing end of the hall, under the gallery, were some warped shelves which were known as *the library*, and on one of these shelves there were some books which were rarely read, though they would sometimes be used as stepping stones when juniors played a bout of *you-can't-touch-the-floor*. With the exception of Southey's *Life of Nelson* which lay among a pile of Thirties *Punches* on the top shelf, most of these books had lost their covers, and their illustrations had either been removed or doctored. Some master, possibly Cleeve, had filled in the titles again on the back of the spines in a fluorescent orange felt-tip. At night the titles glowed in the empty hall, as I imagined the writing had at Belshazzar's feast, and even on dark afternoons the words were as luminous as bougainvillaea flowers in the dusk. I would test my memory by shutting my eyes and seeing if I could remember all of them. As the selection of books and their order rarely altered this exercise had become something of an amulet against the dark, against the woods. To make a mistake would provoke ill luck. The titles went: *Amadis the Lion, Caesar's Punic Wars* [three copies], *Coral Island, The Guns of Navarone* [paperback], *Hereward the Wake, Ieremias Piscator, Island of Sheep, Our Island Story, Ivanhoe, The Magic Bedknob, Mysteries of Easter Island, Papillon* [paperback], *Riddle of the Sands, Rupert of Hentzau, Our Scotland Story, The Silver Sword* [paperback], *A Tale of Two Cities, Vice Versa, We Didn't Mean to Go to Sea* and *The White Cockade*. Of all the titles only three appeared not to be related to islands or water, although if I looked long enough I could begin to notice other connections. When this mnemonic ritual was over I would always run my hands behind the books because sometimes there would be sherbet balls and liquorice sticks hidden in the dust.

On either side of the empty bookcases there were copies of famous pictures of soppy angels and different views of the castle in western Scotland where the school had been evacuated during the war. Sometimes during my rounds I would pause to examine a picture which hung at the foot of the stairs down from the gallery. It was a medieval battle scene, by night. There were rampant hobby-horse chargers and lances lying about like broken pencils on the floor. I imagined that if someone could reach their fingers into the space of the picture and push over one of the knights, all the figures, one after the other, would topple each other down until there was nothing left standing. Under the hibiscus in the front veranda I would arrange my knights like this. Mounted and foot-soldiers, 33:1 and 24:1, die-cast and hand-painted: one tap and they all come tumbling down.

A sagging chicken-wire fence marked the outer boundary of Hobson Wood, or rather that part of the woods which was school property. There was no physical difficulty in crossing this fence. Indeed in some places it had collapsed altogether. Yet there was something fearful about reaching this *ultima Thule* and those boys who stumbled into that small clearing in front of the fence were quick to withdraw again. As the ends of the ancient world had been inhabited by magical beings and mysteries, so those regions beyond the frontiers of Hobson Wood were also populated by legends and superstitions. It was said that a Dornier had come apart in the sky above the beech wood beyond the eastern boundary and the body of the pilot had never been recovered; it was true that one often came across twisted pieces of metal embedded in the ground at the eastern extremes of the wood though there could have been many other explanations for this. If the story was accurate it was likely that the Dornier had been trying to hit the school itself which had been converted into some sort of special command centre in the months leading up to D-Day. Occasionally we still found small lumps of dried sand in the refectory which Musson had told us had been used as the planning room.

On the other edge of the woods, at the western boundary, the trees began to thin out which meant that this section of the woods was rarely used either by quarry or fighters as it afforded such poor cover. From some way behind the perimeter fence we could already see the large clearing which was filled by a rotting elm that had been brought down in a storm some years before. Beyond the broken elm was the ruined house, one side of which was entirely open to the elements, like a doll's house without its façade. One boy had once run over to the house for a dare and fallen through the floor. They kept him in traction for almost a year and when he came out of hospital he had to wear a rubber collar which looked like the type they put on dogs to stop them biting themselves. As ruined houses go the place wasn't up to much, just a stripped-down shell with torn wallpaper flapping in the breeze, and square holes in the walls where the fireplaces had been. The land around the house was said to be haunted by the horse spirit, though there were no signs of any stables in the environs of the house itself. There were ruined stables, however, behind Hobson Lodge which was occupied as a dormitory by different patrols in rotation. Unlike the Grand Guignol mental patients who were said to wander the school buildings, this horse spirit appeared to represent a more immediate kind of threat. Its name consecrated only the most solemn oaths. Whenever the marks of horse-shoes were discovered in the mud around the lodge, the french windows were barricaded with iron beds, and nobody would fall behind the night march down from Sarum Road.

One afternoon I had found myself high on the eastern bank of the woods. From the top of one of the firs on this bank I could see the water-meadows rolled out in the valley below, and the crumpled tablecloth of ancient fortifications on the opposing hills. The previous week I had broken away from Sackville's unit after we had been ambushed a second time. I thought I would hide out at the top of one of the great fir trees and only come down when it began to get dark, but once I had reached the summit I had realized I was fully exposed to look-outs on the opposite banks above the lodge and the camp. Soon after I was on ground-level again I became convinced that there was at least one person following me. Though I couldn't see anything through the dense trunks of the pines and firs, when I stood very still I was sure I could hear twigs breaking somewhere below. I had no choice but to go on; if I changed direction and attempted to cut across westwards I would soon lose my cover. It was not long before I reached the boundary fence: I crouched there for a while on the edge of the narrow clearing looking for fallen branches with which I could hide myself. But there were none large enough. I was certain now that I could hear twigs breaking in at least two different directions beneath me. Then I thought I saw something further down the bank, moving hunched down, flitting between the trunks. Without waiting any longer I ran across the clearing and over the fence.

Nothing seemed to grow under the dark ceiling of the beeches. There was just black mud and rotting leaves and little cover so I kept running until I could no longer see the fence. When I stopped I found myself on the edge of a sort of shallow crater. Nearby, half-buried in the mud, I could see a shard of heavily corroded metal about the size of a tea-tray. One side of it was quite smooth so that I could squat on it and slide down the slopes of the crater. As I tried this from various approaches to see which gave the best ride I became aware that someone was watching me from the branches of one of the surrounding trees. I dropped the sleigh and began to run for it back towards the fence. There was a thud behind me as someone dropped to the ground, and then squelching in the mud as they came after me. It was not easy to run in wellingtons. They kept sliding off and losing their grip on the mud. As I caught sight of the fence through the trees I felt something catch my ankles, and I fell down face-first into the rotting leaves.

'Don't be a mutt, Shady. They'll be waiting for you on the other side.' Ferrers had painted his cheeks and the bridge of his large nose in stripes of mud like a commando. And he had pinched a woolly cap from one of the Moroccans which came down right over his ears. After he had pulled me back to the crater he pressed his sheath knife against my cheek and made me swear on my own life that I would never tell anyone where he had been hiding. Then, perhaps to underscore his point, Ferrers hurled his knife further down the bank after a squirrel, though I saw nothing, and its dirty blade spun an invisible parabola far into the penumbra of the beeches.

'Well, don't just stand there like a dope. Find it, Wopo.' Ferrers wiped his nose with the back of his hand and then gobbed down into the shadowy drop where the knife had fallen.

'What if I funk it?'

'Then I'll bung you over the fence and the Duffer will bury you alive.' Ferrers picked up a twig and flicked it up into the dark canopy of the trees.

'Is this where your base is?'

'Stumm it, dungfeatures, or you'll break our cover.' Ferrers had crouched down at the edge of the crater. He was so still that it was as if I were alone again.

'But do the fighters ever cross the boundary?'

'If they smell a wop they do.'

It was almost dark before we found the knife again.

Late for the march back to the Sarum Road, we clambered up the face of the coomb where the summer play was staged, a scaled-down version of the natural amphitheatre behind Palgrave's house in Somerset where I had spent the previous half-term when my grandmother in Yorkshire had not been well enough to receive me . . . Though it was already dusk when we reached the hills above the house there had still been light enough to make out the celebrated rose-red sheep of which Palgrave was so proud; he claimed they provided the wool for the Saints scarf which bulged out like a cartoon Adam's apple from the buttoned collar of his Burberry. I had been more struck by the strange humpbacked hills, and the unearthly colour in the darkening air, and far below those cetacean hills the black slick of the Bristol Channel under a sky which was like looking at a light through honey.

The following morning, Palgrave's mother, who had piercing beryl eyes and a commanding manner, had sent us off to clean out the tackroom and the smaller stable. Whenever we reported back having finished one task she would immediately send us out on other jobs: mowing the croquet lawn, building fires, lopping trees, mending slow leaks. I had tried to learn each skill as we went along though Palgrave seemed reluctant to lead by example and in each case deferred to my experimental approaches. All the rooms in the house were tall and square. They made one feel so small and asymmetrical. In their old house, Palgrave had explained, the rooms were twice as tall again, but since the place had become the headquarters of MCI Communications all the ceilings had been lowered so that the employees would feel more at home. The wing above the stables where we slept was considerably colder than any of the dormitories, though the beds were some improvement on the convex gridirons to which we had grown accustomed. The principal decoration in my room was an almost life-sized worm-pitted figure of a Negro, with what appeared to be a striped sweatband around his curls, proudly displaying a fading cornucopia of sugar-beet, grapes, tobacco leaves, and pine-apples.

The house rule was no sleeping in during the mornings or you missed breakfast, but as the breakfast was barely distinguishable from what was served in the refectory this did not constitute much of an incentive to rise. I would spend the mornings sneezing out the spores that I had ingested during the course of the night. As a reward, in the evenings after we had completed our labours, we were allowed into the library to watch television, but there was only one channel that wasn't snowed under and that was in Welsh; it had been exciting to see it all the same. At the weekend, when there were guests down from London, we had been sent to amuse ourselves down at the tennis court, a crumbling *En-Tout-Cas* affair, and a beast to fall on. As Palgrave was an ambitious but poor lobber much of the time was spent rooting about for the balls among the cow-dung and the nettles while the mists crept up over the hills from the sea. After we had fought over the extant Penguins and Clubs in the pantry we would be corralled in the tackroom where our dead skins of rose-red mud could flake off harmlessly over the uneven parquetry. Despite the rigours of the place I felt strangely sad to be leaving. On the last night, unable to sleep from the spores, I had put my face to the cold glass and looked up at the silhouettes of the hills, great slippery cetaceans nuzzling each other out in the blue dimness: something in me had wanted suddenly to start out into the hills and be forgotten there in that dark rolling place, and when I could no longer feel my feet I padded back to bed and held myself under the blankets so I wouldn't see the dawn come. And on the drive back the next day, after we had passed Stonehenge, I had pretended not to notice when Palgrave had brought down his *Look & Learn* over his face like a viser so I wouldn't see him blubbing.

The week after our return I had asked Palgrave if he would desert the camp and become a quarry. I had hesitated to ask this, partly because I had heard the rumours about the penalties for desertion, but also because I suspected his disappearance would provoke more elaborate and efficient hunts. When finally I asked him he had avoided my eyes and muttered something about his prospects of becoming a look-out. Already I had wondered what would happen when that day came when he had me square in his sights; though I had heard that the Beaufort brothers had fought on different sides in the woods. In a way I think I was more reassured by the idea of Palgrave in the camp, not out in the woods.

For the first few days after our meeting in the beech wood Ferrers had avoided me, keeping to himself in the dormitory and during breaks. On the Sunday after our meeting I had kept to the western reaches of the wood, honing my tracking skills by stalking the Sackvilles and Barnsley, searching for suitable saplings to work into fighting sticks. On the following Wednesday, however, having again found myself up on the eastern bank, I crossed the chicken-wire fence and headed back to the crater. I discovered Ferrers at the summit of the same tree where I had disturbed him the previous week. He was carving something into one of the highest branches. A sign in the shape of a crossed horse-shoe. 'Even if you fluked your way up to where I just was you'd never in a thousand years understand it,' he sneered as he leapt down on to the palliasse of rotting leaves.

'Can I have a go with your knife?'

'Only if you let me use you as a target first.'

He threw the knife so it scraped the outside rim of my right wellington and stuck up to its handle in the mud. The handle was plastic, made to look like tortoiseshell. I allowed him to demonstrate all his throwing techniques with the margins of my feet as his target zone. First there was the Standard Spin; apparently this was a technique favoured by the Mexicans. Then there was the Flip, used for close-quarters throwing, as in a crowded bar or a circus. There was the Gurkha Underhand, also known as the Commando Swipe, for the element of surprise in a heavy foliage environment. And not forgetting the Disguised Under-hand, for discreet use under tables and in cattle pens. Needless to say by the time he had finished demonstrating

67

all the techniques and their variants it was already growing dark, and too late for me to try my hand.

As the weeks passed Ferrers seemed to have become more scrupulous about avoiding me in the dormitory and during breaks, yet our secret trysts in the beech wood continued. Gradually he opened the stopper and decanted the secret philtre of his knowledge into me, one precious drop at a time, so that the furtive essences of tracking, camouflage, stave fighting and hand-to-hand combat were slowly distilled into my noviciate body. In return Ferrers wanted to know all about camels and sheikhs and dancing-girls. Every day I checked the form papers assiduously in the hope of garnering information on these topics. Apart from the two-cylinder models in Regents' Park my experience of camels was confined to that moth-eaten creature which squatted among the souvenir stalls in Baalbeck with a disdainful expression that reminded my father of Louis MacNeice; this creature would swivel its neck around one hundred and eighty degrees to stare ruminatively at its broad-beamed American passengers before spitting over their slacks. But this was not what Ferrers wanted to hear. Only bloody raids on caravanserai and bold ambuscades by Glubb Pasha's camel corps would satisfy him. Fortunately I had an ample fund of these tales with which Omer had diverted me during those slow climbs through Aley and Bhamdoun to our summer house in the Chouf; occasionally he would break off to fulminate against the donkeys and the wheelbarrow men overladen with water-melons and bananas and the erratic *services* impatient to return to the city to pick up more passengers: I looked forward to this even more than to the stories themselves. One afternoon, crouching as usual on our corroded metal sheets with the rime drip-dripping down through the leaves, Ferrers had begged me to tell him about the guerrillas and terrorists, even promising to show me some tracks left by the horse spirit on the western edge of the woods if I complied, but though I had grown more confident in my story-telling I did not feel my powers of invention were adequate to this new topic until I had done some further research.

despite the curfew

'What's green on the outside and red on the inside and sits in a corner?'

'What?'

'A baby eating razor blades.'

'What goes round and round and is red all over?'

'Ha. That's a baby in a liquidizer.'

Where these jokes began nobody knew for sure. After lights-out they passed in Chinese whispers, from bed to bed, from dormitory to dormitory, and soon they had infected the whole school. As the jokes were disseminated down the school they became transformed into riddles. Those *jun-men* who did not know the answers were dealt out what was known as *Theban treatment* though this appeared indistinguishable from the usual drubbing. Eventually the jokes were declared *stale as shortbread* and anyone caught telling them after this would be banished to Coventry for a week.

After he had languished in Coventry for several weeks in succession Standish had gone around whispering to everyone about the existence of a special vat at the back of the hospital on the Sarum Road which contained all the things sent for incineration. When they were emptying the contents of the vat into the fire, he said, a baby had crawled out alive, and he had it on good information that this baby had been adopted and was now in his second year at North Hill. Ever since it had been discovered that Standish had been assembling an Airfix *Panzerarmee* in the modelling room, where only new men and wets ever went, his stature in the dormitory had gone into a tailspin. When Sackville learned that Standish had been circulating the story about the baby in the incinerator he proclaimed it one of the most stale stories ever (though I had never heard it) and immediately sentenced Standish to a further ten days in Coventry. If someone was discovered communicating with a man in Coventry (no exception was made for play-readings and conversation classes) he was summarily banished there himself. In the wake of the baby–joke craze there had been weeks when more than half the school had been in Coventry, and an uncanny half-silence of rustling and scraping had settled over entire regions of the school.

As the long summer term wore on flash floods of madness had begun to wash over the school, leaving little pools of delirium behind that stubbornly would not dry up or be sluiced away. When the rains suddenly fell out of the blue sky in my city during the summer months all the children along Ain Mreisse would run out on to the streets and the balconies and hold up their hands into the moist sky. But within moments the shower had passed and they would stand and watch the lonely cloud pass far out over the sea as though it were some rogue balloon riding away without them to some distant and fabulous land. Similarly when the summer madness came down over the school some boys would rush out into the open and offer themselves to a full wetting, but there were others who continued about their business with the madness hidden within themselves. We never knew who they were, these conjurers, though everyone had their own suspicions. Stevenson must have had such matters in mind when he wrote of boys who play along a dangerous shore with lanterns tightly buttoned up beneath their coats. The problems all began in the neighbouring dormitory, West, where some Curlews had recently revived an old cult centred around an eye-shaped hole in the floor known as the *Holy of Holies* into which they poured libations of honey and shampoo. It was not long before all our sponge-bags and tuck-boxes were infested by a plague of giant earwigs which had emerged from the hole. We had retaliated by kidnapping two junior Curlews whom we had feasted on earwigs and dispatched in the usual ways. During the following afternoon, however, certain unknown raiders, possibly dissatisfied with the leniency of Sackville's measures, had been spied entering West disguised in pillow cases where they had proceeded to desecrate the venerable hole with sheath knives and dividers.

The same week, though an uneasy truce had held between the two dormitories against which the hotheads chafed on both sides, some lone provocateur (or possibly some small maverick unit) had systematically blocked every bog in the main building, and then flushed until the murky effluence was flowing freely down the stairs, into the corridors, out into the dormitories. Neither Johnny Bunts nor the Moroccans would intervene, and finally external plumbers had to be called to staunch the creeping floods. The next morning, while we were still moving about in wellingtons sniffing the garlic cloves which Sister Gab had distributed, it was found that the pet room adjoining the biology lab had been struck during the night. Several gerbils were discovered to have bled to death as a result of what appeared to have been homespun spaying operations; though no mention was made of this at the time it became known later that an axolotl had also been found skinned and filleted but still twitching. Despite the relentless punishment parades and the cancellation of all weekend privileges the lantern-bearers continued their lonely work. At Sunday evensong, normally attended by visiting parents, it caught the attention of the chapel prefect that the plain wooden altar cross had been tampered with. A closer inspection revealed that the words *JC woz here* had been crudely carved along the transept of the cross.

A week of false fire-alarms, further bog-blocking, and damage to the cricket square had culminated on Friday morning with the discovery of the headman's Peugeot estate nose down in the diving end of the swimming pool. It took the tow-truck five hours to winch it out due to the counter-weight of the water: the same day it was announced that swimming was to be replaced by punishment parades for the remainder of the year. Sports Day itself would only be reprieved when the culprits came forward and confessed. I was secretly relieved.

Sometimes during the long parades there was the peace to pray, and I would find myself back in the garden again. *I am watching Emmy from the vantage of the hibiscus over the veranda whose pink trumpets camouflage my crimson alligator shirt; in such a garden the boldest colours are the most discreet. She has kicked off her sneakers, and heedless of the scorpions and serpents she creeps barefoot through the long grass. Her loyal salukis, though bothered by the heat, stay close to her side. Catching the sunlight, her crescent-moon hairclip flashes Indian signals across the overexposed gardens. Everywhere she walks the land is drowned in light. The sun protects her and blinds her enemies. And as the evening draws on we go up to the flat terrace at the top of the house which is still strung with white streamers and dried-up sprays of asphodels from the last dance which nobody has bothered to bring in. She likes to pluck off the desiccated petals and grind them to dust in her little fist. We fight over who will have the binoculars to scan for sea monsters and submarines out in the bay. Emmy always has a different explanation as to why the water suddenly changes colour a couple of miles out, from blue-green into deep blue. This time she claims her long-haired brother Trench has it on good authority that the blue-green water has been dyed by giant poisonous squids which have been deliberately released into the shallows by the government to protect the shore against an alien landing. When I hear this I chase her down into the hammock which hangs in the branches of the cedar in the lower gardens, the one that doesn't like the sea, and I spin her over and over until she is trapped like a seal in a net. She lets me do this because she knows she will be able to get me in trouble for it later. For the same reason she is persuaded to climb the precipice outside the drive and deftly slips down and cuts her knee. If the cut is not impressive enough she grins up at me and picks away a little more skin. When her driver comes she smears her honey face with spittle and runs into the silent house to look for my mother, throwing her plaintive holler through the empty, brightly lit rooms. 'Hey-ey, Mrs Shadrach. Tobias bees mean. Tobias bees mean. He bees mean.' As if she were practising her scales.*

There was little else to do during the long parades other than day-dream and plot and fiddle. My place was right at the back corner of the gym beside Ferrers, just behind the window which was blind from accumulated grime, and covered in wire-netting to guard against balls. This was one of the most sought-after spots during parades as it was almost entirely concealed from Magyar who was perched up in the gallery on his shooting stick; there was also the added benefit of a back-rest in the form of the rubbed-smooth wall bars. If I got there first I bagged a place for Ferrers, and usually he did the same for me. If Standish stopped shielding him from the master Ferrers would give him a sharp clip on the ankles. The rest of the time Ferrers just desultorily scuffed the backs of Standish's shoes so Standish would not forget that he was providing valuable cover.

Some diversion was provided by a hairy medicine ball which would roll about lugubriously between patrols. The idea was to arouse the attention of Magyar, who dozed flamingo-style on his shooting stick, at the precise moment that the ball was at the feet of some particular rival who would then be hauled off to the headman. Most boys coped with the doldrums of the parades by retreating into private reveries and secret games of solitaire whose rules were almost never divulged. The parades spawned a craze for miniaturization. As the weeks dragged on and all visiting privileges continued to be suspended the trading value of matchboxes, ball-bearings and Blue-Tack began to spiral; I heard of sheath knives being exchanged for pocket mazes, catapults for pipe-cleaners. In the back row Barnsley would work an elaborate sortilege using fingernails and toothbrush bristles. Bass did *netsuke* on a drawer-knob. Savage waged bitter campaigns on the palms of his hands with tiny balls of blotting paper, chewing up the vanquished. Meanwhile, on the other side, I would watch Palgrave shuffle and cut the same eleven Saints cards over and over again while he stared out through the blind window, never looking down at the card he had drawn. I liked to think he was dreaming of that forgotten kingdom of whale-backed hills and carnelian sheep which one day he would rule as he pleased.

Privately I gave thanks to those who still carried the madness hidden within themselves. The parades had become a slow-motion sanctuary in a world that was turning increasingly hostile and unpredictable. Only the week after Ferrers had questioned me about the guerrillas, I had arrived at the beech wood to find Duff-Revel and some lesser fighters squatting nonchalantly around the edges of the crater. My capture seemed to give them no pleasure. I had been herded back to the camp with what appeared to be staves of my own making; only the pervading dampness and the uneven wind had discouraged them from hog-tying me over one of the scouting fires. After the fighters had tired of wanding me I had been set to

78

slopping out one of the inner tunnels which had been flooded by the recent rains. I slushed about in the earthy darkness sustained only by visions of Ferrers rising like an avenging angel from the pits to rout the fighters and scatter them into the woods. Afterwards I discovered Ferrers had never been captured. He had stonily refused to explain how he had escaped. He had calculated that his secret might easily be prized out of me, an oyster from a throw-away shuck. My single consolation was that I had been spared the humiliation of having Palgrave witness my distress at the hands of the fighters, though later I had to sit through all his sullen blandishments.

But my capture had been overshadowed by another potentially more far-reaching disaster. Taking advantage of the general confusion in the wake of the outrages, Duff-Revel had sought to establish a new system of earthworks within the immediate vicinity of the school itself. Using the same logic that places vice houses in close proximity to the local gendarmerie in many European cities, Duff-Revel had chosen to situate his new enterprise in that rectangle of wasteground lying not twenty yards from the masters' lodge, bordered to the south and east by the old town gasworks, a giant wind section of bulbous tubes and cylinders skulking behind the horse-chestnuts along the boundary fence. Within only a few days a shallow network of dug-outs and connecting culverts had sprung up, and a new labour force, seduced by the promise of hard wages, was already at work shifting soil and rubble from the tunnels into mounds above the slough of puddles and ditches. These new dug-outs, unlike the mines in the woods, were surface constructions lined with polythene and roofed with scraps of corrugated iron weighted down with bricks and tin cans filled with water. The tunnels linking these holes were only deep enough not to be disturbed by light surface activity, and tapered down in the middle sections to no more than a couple of feet across. Close up the place came across as grubby and unformidable, a twin town to the water-logged settlements which had spread out along the the airport road from Chatila where Omer's family lived, the shacks too low to stand in, let alone the lean-tos, their tin roofs held down against the wind with breeze blocks and old cans of Nido. However the makeshift appearance of the new camp was deceptive. For from the vantage of the old air-raid shelters we could look down on the works and make out a certain overall shape which was beginning to emerge from beneath all the puddles and the rubble. Clearly Duff-Revel was working to some kind of plan: crude revetments, redoubts, and shallow buttresses were starting to link up together to form a coherent stellar arrangement. Those who had not been induced to work in the new camp idled about on its edges, gaping, commentating, pretending to inside information on the final design of the work. But both the workers and the observers could only speculate as to the precise nature of this new enemy which Duff-Revel had contrived so emphatically to defend himself from.

These were the weeks that everyone dreamt of sappers and catacombs, though at any other time these preoccupations were rarely far from the surface of our lives. During those sparse breaks unconsumed by the punishment parades all the talk was of the sewers of Paris, the caves of the Hobbit, the way of the Golem under Prague. It was during these weeks that I first told Ferrers of the networks of secret arsenals and shooting-ranges hidden under the refugee camps. At first he did not seem interested. But later I found him in the trunk room making diagrams of what I had invented.

Overnight Standish was back in favour. It was rumoured he was in possession of a map of the secret web of fall-out tunnels under Moscow. Opinion was divided, however, on the authenticity of this item, and, after Sackville refused to raise a ransom to free back the map from the Curlews who had apparently stumbled upon it rolled up in the fuselage of a Dornier during a routine search of the modelling room, the majority dismissed the map as a fake. Legends of tunnels under the school itself also enjoyed a revival during this period. The old story of a tunnel whose mouth was said to lie under the base of the war memorial in the rose garden began to attract the interest of even the most sceptical among us, and every break there would be boys with forked sticks and other divining devices tracking the route of the putative tunnel across the croquet lawn and through the upper gardens. Some claimed the tunnel came out somewhere under the Music School, others that it continued under the Sarum Road and emerged in the cellars of Hobson Lodge. Such was the interest in the tunnel that Bass and other junior Curlews paid out undisclosed sums to Barnsley and Sackville in the expectation of being shown the concealed entrance under the lodge only to be dealt a thorough wanding and abandoned in the locked cellars; they were later released by an off-duty matron who had come down to investigate the banging.

It was during the height of this mania for tunnels that Duff-Revel led a raid which would become the subject of much later confusion and popular distortion, and would eventually occasion a series of *gestes* almost as far-fetched as those that told of the exploits of his older cousin whose presence still hovered over the school though he had left over a decade before, going on to bite the ear off a Popper and then vanish into the jungles of Honduras. What is more or less clear is that Duff-Revel, along with Douglas, Beaufort, and other fighters, had managed to crawl beneath the floorboards, passing under the matron's room and the entire length of North, before emerging in West at precisely that moment when the majority of senior Curlews were engaged in offering libations over their recently desecrated hole. It appears that an agent on the inside had already loosened the requisite floorboards in West to facilitate the surprise assault. There is little consensus about what followed, but what is certain is that many of the Curlews were so shaken by whatever took place during the attack that they refused to speak about what had occurred even long after Duff-Revel had left the school. The following morning, cowed and heavily trademarked, most of the Curlews reported to the new camp for work assignments in what had clearly been agreed the previous night as part of the terms of their surrender. From this time on Duff-Revel's patrol and the Curlews would effectively operate as a single and united force. Later Ferrers confided to me that he believed Duff-Revel had derived his tactical inspiration for the raid from the Egyptian Yom-Kippur offensive at Suez. I was quietly sceptical about this, however, because I knew Duff-Revel never read the papers.

I had spent the afternoon before the raid on the Curlews off games, reading in the Green Room behind Milton. Like a lot of the rooms in the school the Green Room wasn't really used for anything much. Nor was it unused exactly. Such places were occupied infrequently but specifically. The Green Room, for example, served as a transit point for props and scenery which were normally stored in one of the creosoted ex-army huts, but in the summer the place was more or less empty and undisturbed. The trick, if one can call it that, was to *shirk* shirking by mingling with those going into the changing rooms after lunch, and thus avoid all the other shirkers who had slunk off to spend their afternoon ragging in the old bog-houses and the Music School cubicles. Shirkers rarely came down to the Green Room.

When I heard Cleeve's rubber-soled shuffle outside the

door I knew already he would want to savour fully my reason for not being on the sick list (he said he collected excuses of which he was going to publish a book one day). Then he would send me off to write ten sides on the inside of a ping-pong ball (he collected these also) or stand in the lower corridor to face the wall of old boys for the rest of the afternoon. But he just waited there by the door in his old fawn waistcoat with the mother-of-pearl buttons which echoed his filmy eyes, running his fingers absent-mindedly through his thick pomaded hair, regarding me with a look of facetious expectation. The secret with Cleeve was to confect an excuse that was both elegant and ludicrous enough to surprise him: not an easy task at short notice.

'Sir . . . Er.'

'And may I enquire what you are reading indoors on this balmy afternoon?'

'This, sir.' I held up the book. He pretended to register surprise, and then narrowed his nacreous eyes to denote a measure of cod complicity. As he turned and closed the door I caught the draught of his breath across my face. It had the same dead-sweet smell that hung around the bottom of the drive at home which came not from the terraced carob trees but from the beds of pitcher plants and the unstirring beakers of dead insects between their swollen franges. *It was there that I would wait in the evenings while Omer shammied down the Plymouth or leant against the bonnet reading As Safir or my father's copy of the Herald Tribune. I always hoped that one day he would ask me what one of the English words meant but he never did. One night he had become so disgusted with what he had been reading that he had kicked the paper into the ground and spat on it. When I asked him why he was so angry he refused to explain and peered up towards the mountains, blinking and rubbing his blue crusader eyes as if he had just stepped out into a khamsin. That morning I had watched as he had walked right up to the front line of students demonstrating with placards and megaphones outside the gates and*

83

drawn an invisible line along the ground with the tip of his boot and then waited to see if anyone would cross. Omer had a low opinion of students, and whenever he had to drive through one of their flimsy barricades he would call them pansy-richboys and dogs-not-men to their faces. A few moments after Omer had drawn his invisible line the Squad 16 men had arrived in their black Chevrolet shooting-brakes and the students had dispersed back up the hill to the various faculty buildings they were occupying.

When I saw my mother and father come down from the veranda I crept back behind the carob trees so they would not see me. Omer was wearing his peaked green cap which meant they were probably going to one of the embassies or the St Georges. Those were the evenings my mother would wear her long backless dresses which glinted in the tail-lights of the Plymouth and rustled like someone crawling through dry grass. Sometimes the following day I would climb into her deep wardrobe and try to find the dress she had been wearing and brush my hands and cheeks against it. You could never tell by looking at them what they were going to feel like.

reports of an incident

For reasons of his own my father keeps a dried snakeskin in a shoe-box on top of the tall bookcase in his siesta room where the persiennes are always drawn to keep the heat at bay. To reach the box I pile the All England Law Reports against the wall and clamber up, the dusty concertina of pages warped by sea travel puffing out invisible clouds of spores so my eyes begin itching, and I have to grimace tightly to stop my head exploding into sneezes. When I am the same height as the box I ease the lid away and peek in. The skin is bone-grey and nothing like a snake, more like a discarded honeycomb with its brittle hexagonal scales. Something I have never seen has slipped away leaving behind this crisp rusk, and it is this lack of snakeness that discomforts me and draws me back to visit it. Every time Elias the gardener comes upon one of these skins behind the bougainvillaeas or on the lifeless overwatered earth of the carob terraces there is hysteria in the kitchens, more even than when an Abu Brace has been sighted in one of the bedrooms or the General Electric has come free of its moorings and begun hobbling out across the floor. Mona and Lamia will only venture out on to the back porch wearing my mother's wellington and cuisses improvised from plastic bags until the snake-catcher comes and carries the thing off writhing in a hessian sack. Though it will only be a matter of weeks before another skin is found, and again I will climb up to the box and ask myself what sort of a thing is this which slips from matter to matter like a lost soul.

But now that the term had begun again I felt oddly ashamed for having asked myself such questions. I try not to think of the summer and when I do I see it jumbled up and unfocused, a pack of old slides, the colours already bleeding, withdrawing. *Salzburg. Lake Geneva. Lausanne. Lakes, mountains, forests, hotels called castles, castles called hotels, the air so clear I want to put my hand out of the window and stroke the banks of trees which are so many shades of green that green could have been the only colour in the world and we would have been no poorer. And there was that curious sensation of waking in a giant bed, stretching in every direction without finding a limit, not knowing which way up, which way round, the world is. And every day another slightly different Wiener Schnitzel with its circumcised black olives-rolled-in-anchovies, another île flotant, another mille-feuille which always betrays its promise.* But now that the term was upon me once more it was as if all these impressions belonged to someone else entirely. They were lodged inside me like some exotic cargo which must be jettisoned if the ship is to ride out the storm ahead.

The Sunday-morning service in chapel would usually be conducted by visiting clergymen and itinerant worthies. The previous week there had been a missionary who ran a school for coloureds out in Rhodesia; these were not orphans but the children and grandchildren of mixed couplings. The missionary passed around photographs of the children standing in front of the school buildings with forced smiles on their faces. At the end there had been a lot of questions about how precisely a coloured was distinguished from a black, and what exactly a Kaffir was, but no one seemed to be interested in why the coloureds had to go to a school of their own. After the questions there was a collection. We all wrote down an amount of money on scraps of paper and put them back into one of the knitted purses that had been made by Sister Gab. The practice of giving everybody coins before the service had been quickly discontinued. Throughout the week photographs of the coloured school had been going the rounds of the dormitories accumulating scholia.

The week before, Harvest Festival, the Sunday service had been taken by a band of evangelicals in cheesecloth blouses with guitars and tambourines. Everbody was expected to link hands and join in the chorus. The trick was to surprise your neighbour into making a disruption, especially if he was being taken out, either by heeling him in the shins or boring into the palm of his hand with a thumbnail cultivated for this purpose. There was always a fair crop of solitary paraders on those Sundays the evangelicals took the service.

When I asked Ferrers why his parents never came to chapel he said this was because they weren't religious. This week Ferrers was reading the lesson. This was not the first time Ferrers had been chosen but he hoped it would be the last. Only boys who were being taken out were selected. Ferrers' parents would be waiting for him after the service reading the Sunday papers in their old-fashioned Volvo.

Only his head and neck are visible above the scrolled rim of the lectern. He does not look up from the page and pretend to be seeing what he is describing at the back of the room as we have been taught to do. If he has brushed his hair it doesn't show. His hair is thick and wiry, almost African, like horse-hair stuffing, brushing-resistant. I cannot help noticing again, looking up at him from this angle with his head down over the lectern, how there is some aspect to his face which is strange precisely because it is familiar, as if I had glimpsed it everywhere before I came to the school, but without recognizing what I did not yet know. It is as though my own face was there behind his, masked over, and his buried behind mine. He reads flatly, without expression:

> Then flew one of the Seraphim unto me,
> having a live coal in his hand,
> And he laid it upon my mouth
> (He wipes his mouth quickly with the back of his hand)
> And said, Lo, this hath touched mine lips,
> And thine iniquity is taken away, and thy sin purged.
> Also I heard the voice of the Lord saying
> (He disappears completely behind the lectern. His diction accelerating, a sprint finish),
> Whom-shall-I-send, and-who-will-go-for-us?
> Then-said-I, Here am I: Send me.
> Here-endeth-the-lesson.

Before everyone stands to sing the next hymn he closes the Bible which makes a loud plopping sound.

Palgrave's parents have come in late with his older sisters and are sitting at the back under the organ. One of his sisters (both of whose existence Palgrave long denied) is reading something on her lap, and the other is looking out of the window. Her distracted but deathly-still profile against the darkening sky reminds me of the grieving ladies carved from eggshell onyx and mounted on dark velvet in my grandmother's hall. On the morning we left Palgrave's house his sisters had arrived from their convent to begin their own half-term. I had almost expected them to appear in sandals, long gowns and wimples, like the Sisters of St Maroun who took in Omer's brother after he became convinced the crows above his camp were Israeli spies and let loose at them with his AK47. But when they arrived they were wearing spangled sunglasses and hipster

90

jeans with chunky silver buckles, and they ran shrieking up to their rooms and never came down again, not even to see Palgrave off.

After chapel is over those parents who live too far away to return home will take their sons and their sons' friends down to the Royal Hotel in town for Sunday lunch. There they will eat over-cooked roast and frozen vegetables under impasto seascapes and talk in whispers because the tables are a little too close, while the boys, still in their Sunday suits but with loosened collars, will cast furtive glances across the underlit room at each other's families. The sons are tense and doubly vigilant. At any moment either their parents or their friends may say something which will betray them. Mostly it is the parents and the friends who make conversation while the sons pretend to look out of the french windows to the end of the croquet lawn where, under the moss-encrusted statuary, all the dogs are romping together.

For the third time this week broken glass has turned up on the lower games pitches. Yobs from the town have been blamed. Musson and Magyar are talking of mounting night patrols along the boundary fence. But the rumours from the Curlews are that Duff-Revel and Douglas have been testing a new device which they plan to deploy at the new camp above the masters' lodge. Standish even claims to know the design of the weapon and has been negotiating with Sackville all week to trade the secret for certain undisclosed favours. According to Ferrers, Duff-Revel and Douglas have managed to pick the lock of the chemistry cupboard and have begun experimenting with devices constructed from a sealed jam jar filled with water and quantities of sodium and potassium. (When Commander Wingate slices into the bar of sodium during a class demonstration the inside of the bar is the colour of boiled chicken liver. Like a mad fly against a pane the crumb-sized pellet fizzles around and around in the

water until all that remains is a faint evanescent scum.)
Towards the end of the service the headman improvises a
prayer on the subject of the broken glass; this is principally
for the benefit of the parents at the back. It follows familiar
enough lines:

> Oh Lord, please forgive those who are impressionable,
> And are easily fooled by the bad example of those around them,
> And are led astray by evil films,
> And whose unhappy lives tempt them to harm others more fortunate
> than themselves.
> Amen.

Beneath the gourds and wheatsheafs and sprays of dried
flowers left over from Harvest Festival, the fruit in the
wicker baskets is beginning to shrivel and harden. It gives
off the same shrunk-fruit scent that hangs around the
sideboard in so many of the dining rooms of England,
the scent of afternoon card games and little conversation.
Old Maid. Whist. Canasta. Not a dead smell but a dying one
. . . I look up to the Annunciation hanging above the vestry.
The angels bobbing in the empyrean wiggle about like the
swimmers at the Phoenicia. *We watch them through the porthole
from the underground bar. They shimmy and twirl and somersault
underwater, squash their bodies up against the glass, play dead lying
face-down on the surface of the pool. My father tells me that the
swimmers are hired from Europe, from Austria, to entertain the
guests. He chuckles with fixed lips, with his Voltaire smile, his smile
of reason. Perhaps he believes the guests are fools for enjoying this
sort of entertainment, or fools for believing that these are casual
swimmers, or that Monsieur S., the hotel's owner, is a fool for
providing such swimmers. There is sure to be a fool in it somewhere.
Monsieur S. is one of the richest men in a city full of rich men. Every
time his name is mentioned the same stories follow after as if they
were attached to his name by golden chains. How he made his*

fortune among the desert Arabs exchanging one gold sovereign bearing the King's head for two bearing the Queen. How the walls of his palace are lined with Gauguins and Renoirs. How his wine cellars are powdered with dust imported from Bordeaux. But these achievements do not exempt him from being a fool in my father's eyes: on the contrary they seem to be qualifications. So much so in fact that whenever my sister has been visiting the daughter of Monsieur S. she is invited that same evening to join my parents at dinner, and I hear their laughter coming up through the kitchens, and the silences in between, as if the house were catching its breath: sometimes when the laughter has stopped I will hear the Phoenician glass humming to itself in the tall cabinets beneath my room. And whenever we have guests from London or America my father never fails to mention that my sister walks home from Monsieur S.'s house all on her own in the dark through the streets of the safest city in the world. Though really my sister prefers to come back riding on the front seat of the Plymouth with Omer. He always wears his peaked green cap in her honour but before they set out she knocks it off and hides it under the seat.

After the Phoenicia we drive Emmy back to her house. When we arrive her brother Trench is sitting sucking pomegranates on the veranda with his drop-out friends, Marlin and Judge, spitting the seeds out over the terracotta tiles. Trench doesn't qualify as a drop-out because he is still studying medicine at the AUB. But he looks just the same as his friends: scarab beads, jeans cut off above the knee, washed-out T-shirts, sweatbands on their wrists and bunching up their hair, and that squinting sun-dazed look, although they are always sitting in the shade. Omer stares at them through the tinted window the same way he stares out the students behind the barricades, as if they were something he wouldn't even trample in. As I follow Emmy up to the veranda her salukis trot out to greet her, their dusty fetlocks lifting in the breeze coming up from the corniche.

Nothing much ever happens at Emmy's, but that nothing much is everything exotic and sophisticated I crave. TV, comics

93

(Mad, DC and Marvel while I am only allowed Tintin and sometimes Asterix), bubble-gum, peanut-butter-and-jelly, posters, pop music. I follow entranced as she trails her way listlessly from room to room; picking up something only to discard it again; calling for a snack from the kitchens only to nibble and abandon it; ordering a cupboard to be unpacked only to forget what it was she had lost. Days at Emmy's pass as convoluted and weightless as the rings of smoke from the gently bubbling hookah which makes its measured rounds out on the veranda, while the maid, like a faithful votary, constantly nourishes the little god with brass tongfuls of red-hot charcoal flakes.

Emmy and I are under strict instructions never to enter Trench's den at the top of the house. Not even Emmy's parents are allowed in the den, but today, for reasons that he keeps to himself, Trench lets us peek in. There is a sticker of a death's head on the door, and a sign in Gothic script which says Dead Surfers. Normally this is as far as we come. There is no furniture in the den, just bean-bags and cushions along the walls, an old gramophone in the corner, and a cluster of hookahs and pipes and bronze Damascus ashtrays in the middle of the floor. I am a little disappointed. I had expected something more. The walls have been painted black, but one area is still white where they must have run out of paint. On the wall there is a poster of the marines raising the flag at Iwo Jima. I recognize the photography from one of my father's history books. Over it someone has painted a black peace sign in ellipsis, as if it were a bent hoop, lolloping along.

'Wow. It's like the Bat Cave,' I say, wanting to show that I know about television.

'Kind of,' Emmy replies. Then Marlin sniggers, and Trench and Judge begin sniggering too. I try to put a brave face on it.

'Don't you think Marlin laughs like Mutley?' I say to Emmy.

'Yeah. I guess.' She sounds unconvinced.

'Which side of the door are the Surfers?' I ask no one in particular.

'Both sides.' They all three say this at the same time.

94

The TV is on in the background. There are the same old pictures of Hueys buzzing over the jungle canopy while the announcer patters on in his affected Maronite French. Trench is shooting at the screen with a Colt 45 cap-gun. There are no caps in the gun so he makes his own firing sound POWW POWW *and then blows away the pretend-smoke from the end of the muzzle like Lucky Luke.*

'Hey, Tobo,' says Marlin, 'you want to smoke — ain't nothing to it but to do it.' He offers me a long carved pipe covered with silver anaglyphs, silk tassels hanging down from the bowl. He is grinning like a cartoon Mexican, then wider, like Mutley himself. I can hear the horn of the Plymouth outside, short, long, then short again. Omer is waiting. As I run outside I stop in the veranda as usual to pick up the pomegranate seeds from the warm tiles.

Fruit trees had sown themselves all along the roadside, across the mountains from Baabda to Chtaura. There were apple trees, vines creeping over the rocks, ancient date palms, pear trees: figs, quinces, acadiniah, wild cherries. Sometimes we would stop the car and pick the fruit of that season along the roadside, bringing back baskets to be sorted and washed. Omer said that all the trees had grown up from seeds spat out by passing travellers.

When I returned I went down to the lower gardens where the grass was long under the seasick cedar tree and sowed my pomegranate seeds as I always did when I returned from Emmy's. First I put them in my mouth, being careful not to chew and break them, then I spit the dragon's teeth out into the long grass. When I was younger I had expected something to shoot up immediately the seeds fell to the ground. I would wait, shut my eyes, turn my back, and pray for something to happen. But after being disappointed many times and thinking I must be doing it wrong, I began to believe that maybe what grew from the seeds was only visible to certain people, or at certain special moments, or visible only if I forgot completely that I had sown them.

For some time now I had stopped believing there was anything magical in the seeds but I still sow them in the lower gardens.

Every time I go there I am directing bloody technicolour epics. I am telling myself stories. Like the juniors who play on the banks under the horse-chestnuts I raise up the dead only to mow them down again. Victorious armies are brought low by cunning ambuscades, their supply lines cut, their command structures paralysed: in disorderly retreats they are picked off by minutemen, straggling units mopped up by roving irregulars. History is reversed, rendered synchronic, simultaneous: the armies of every epoch colliding, alliancing, mutating, blending. All the conquerors who once inscribed and hacked their names in steles, in cuneiform, and in delinquent graffiti on the rocks of the Dog River: the hordes of Nebuchadnezzar, Alexander and his Macedonians, Marcus Caracalla's Gallic Legions, Assyrians, Arabs, Crusaders, Turks, French, Australian Light Armour, all are pincered and outflanked and cut down to size by one another; then, bearing the trophies of their own ruin, the survivors are led in a triumph through the bedizened streets of the southern suburbs by fedayeen, comitadji, minutemen, drenched in rice and rose-water and festooned with bunting and white crêpe, as if they had all come down from a wedding in the mountains.

I am watching with Emmy and Trench from the flat roof as the marines come ashore below the corniche. Instead of finding girls in bikinis and urchins selling Coca-Colas, as they did last time around, they are wading straight into another Iwo Jima. There are bold arquebusiers and dead surfers and sharpshooters waiting for them. Helmets are bobbing in the water like lobster pots. The tide is turning dark. Those that make it on to the beach are discovering that the warm sands are mined. They crawl forward on their hands and knees brushing the sand tenderly from side to side as if they were at a dig. Those chosen few who made it beyond the sands have slumped down behind the sea wall where the fierce Ain Mreisse fishermen in their funnel-shaped caps sell hake and red mullet at dawn. There is no way back. Their ships are as small as toys on the horizon. They will have to shoot their way out.

As I am telling myself this story an Israeli Phantom, a real one,

96

breaks the sound barrier somewhere above the mountains. I catch it for a moment, between the clouds, a little silver fish reflecting back the sun. People like to say they decorate the sky. At night we have the stars and in the day we have the fighters which are almost as beautiful: that's what they say.

intelligence sources suggest

We were forbidden to have matches, sweets, torches, sheath knives, comics, bangers (or any other fireworks), gassy drinks, radios, more than three Parkers, and money. All these items were subject to immediate confiscation by prefects, patrol leaders and masters. It was not uncommon for patrol leaders to hold auctions of confiscated and raided articles, or ransom prized possessions such as crystal radios and walkie-talkies back to their owners only to confiscate them again at a later date. Sackville was particularly practised at this type of informal taxation. More exotic items such as radio-controlled cars, kites, and Subuteo, which were occasionally introduced by optimistic new men, would never be put to their intended use but would circulate as spoil from one strong-man to another and from one patrol to the next, until eventually they were sold back to their original owner or taken off to the masters' lodge. Standish claimed that there was a locked attic in the lodge chock-a-block with generations of contraband: whole trunks brimming with catapults, bangers, torches, knives, as far as the eye could see. He claimed his father had seen the place once when he was a boy.

Each outlawed article had spawned its own culture, with

attendant specializations and rituals. Torches, for example, were the subject of fierce competition. Strength and accuracy of beam were prized, as were those pocket torches which came disguised as fountain pens, key-rings and cigarette lighters. The most popular model was a long black Ever Ready with rubber ridges along the length of it which doubled as a cosh or *clobber stick*. This was the model favoured by Sackville for interrogations. The end would be inserted over the eye-socket of the victim so that even if he screwed his eye tightly shut the beam would still penetrate. As he reeled back blinded he would be dealt a quick drubbing over the head.

The most common use of torches was for reading under the blankets after lights-out. This was perhaps the closest we ever came to pure solitude, though for many the principal attraction of reading after lights-out had more to do with clandestine use of a torch than the pleasure of reading; often there would be offenders discovered with torches on under their bedclothes but no reading matter. The readers were usually marked out by a pale aureole above their beds. There were some, however, who never betrayed the presence of their torches, like the lantern-bearers on the dark shore.

The three-Parker rule also provoked elaborate competition. Figures like Bass and Savage would swagger about with up to seventeen Parkers lined up along the inner breast pockets of their jackets. When someone passed they would flash open both flaps like a wideboy knocking out watches. Once I saw Bass pulled up for this by Musson and told to empty out both his pockets. It turned out he only had three full pens on him. The rest were just tops. The question of the clip, the *flèche*, was of utmost significance. On the older Parker 51s the quill and arrowhead, whether in gold or silver, were naturalistically moulded, almost sculpted, while on the recent models the arrow was flat and crudely rendered. The older 51s came in senatorial, world-weary, limousine shades: mulberry, charcoal, mellow claret. The newer models were pseudo-Funky, sudden pinks and pistachio greens, or middle-management co-ordinates: maroon, russet, margarine beige: V-neck colours. Nothing carried less dignity than a cheap Parker, not even an inky Osmeroid or a scratchy Platignum. Some boys tried to circumvent the three-Parker rule by branching out into streamlined Watermans and chunky Shaeffers but these never commanded the same degree of respect as a big-timer 51.

Catapults were the scourge of the balsa-wood gliders launched from the balcony of the pavilion. Those gliders with wider wingspans rarely survived beyond their maiden flight. A conspiracy of silence hung over the workshop where the new men would labour several months on the construction of these gliders, stencilling out struts, props and fuselage panels from sheets of balsa as fine as communion wafer, stretching the tissue over the tender endoskeleton, varnishing the wings until they were as taut as drumskins, only to have the craft plucked from their trembling fingers on the day of its completion. Such planes would be bunged off the balcony farded in Durafix, a thin wisp of smoke trailing in their wake, the flames hardly visible against the sky.

Conkers, ideally hardened on the hot pipes, were the preferred ammunition for the catapults, though pebbles from the drive and dry mud cruds would also do, and rubber balls were used for ricochet effects, to get around corners. Catapults afforded one of the commonest methods of defence during raids. We would practise against the plastic bathroom mugs lined up on a chest at one end of the dormitory. Ferrers always hit the most mugs. His rate of fire was quickest too. Before his target had even fallen he had already loaded again from the breast pockets of his Clydella pyjamas which were always stocked with hardened conkers.

He would practise against light bulbs, pigeons, gliders, torches, passing cars and cyclists. He could knock a Peak Frean out of your fingers at twenty yards and intercept the trajectory of a cricket ball and bring down more choice conker pods from the spreading horse-chestnut trees.

All contraband, any article vulnerable to confiscation, could be swapped on the open market which fluctuated sharply depending on seasonal factors, crazes, sudden scarcities due to mass confiscations, and sudden surfeits following weekends and holidays. All such items would also constitute stakes in games of poker and rummy. A secluded and sound-proof location was required for these games. Usually one of the practice cubicles in the Music School was chosen. It was to these rooms that boys would go if they wanted to light the sprays from aerosols or smoke the headman's Players. The doors could be blocked by sliding across the piano. The walls were lined with thick cardboard and there were egg-boxes on the ceiling. When a player ran out of stakes and money he could concede trademarks. These could be delivered at the time, or deferred and sold through a broker, who, if he had been keeping his ears open, might know of a particular purchaser willing to pay a high price for such rights. These brokers (Savage in our dormitory, and Bass among the Curlews) tended to operate under the direct protection of patrol leaders who would oversee their dealings, enforce trademarkings if required, and extract the cream of the brokers' stock of contraband for their own use.

Greek was taught around a long mahogany table in a hall at one end of the lower corridor. This hall was known as the headman's dining room though no food was ever consumed there. The hall was the meeting place of the Correspondent

Society which was presided over by the headman and convened each week on a Wednesday evening. All the members of this non-voluntary society were expected to report on their chosen specialities, having monitored the form newspapers over the course of the week and extrapolated all relevant information. The headman chain-smoked his way through the proceedings, clawing at his Player, cupping it with butt-stained fingers against some imaginary wind, emphatically rubbing out the stubs into an aluminium ashtray looted from some roadside *estaminet* as if he were struggling to erase some stubborn pasquinade. It was the privilege of the older members of the Correspondent Society to bag all the dull nothing-to-report subjects, New Zealand, Canada, Oceanography and the like, while others opted for juicer material such as Uganda, Nazi Hunters and the IRA. This tactic was somewhat self-defeating, however, as shunned topics such as the Energy Crisis and Industrial Relations would be left to the headman, and he would froth and foam his way through *the inflationary impact of quadrupled oil prices* and *the three-day week* while all around him bodies began to slide inexorably downwards; those who had arrived late and had to sit up the headman's end of the table would find themselves well within range of the spray.

Naturally everyone was surprised when Ferrers volunteered to join the Correspondent Society. As far as anyone could remember nobody had actually volunteered to join the society before. There had to be a catch in it somewhere, but, despite some theories from Standish, nobody could work out what this might be. When the society next convened the headman made quite a performance of introducing Ferrers, *our new correspondent*, as if he were some distinguished visitor come down amongst us. 'And now, Ferrers, what will you be reporting on? On what will you enlighten us?'

Ferrers scratched at one of the leather patches on his jacket. For a moment I thought, probably we all thought, he was going to say something witty and defiant, something that would explain the mystery of his presence. But all he said was, '. . . er. Terrorism. Sir.'

'And would that be Arab terrorism? The Baader-Meinhof? The Red Army Faction? Black Panthers? White Panthers? The Angry Brigade? The Weathermen perhaps?'

'Just Arab, sir.' Everyone looked suitably disappointed. At least some of the correspondents would be relieved of the responsibility of having to report terrorist incidents that occurred within their normally dormant territories. Only two weeks before Stobart, our Benelux correspondent and a nothing-to-report-this-week man, had failed to notice that a BA flight from Beirut had been hijacked over Yugoslav airspace and forced to land at Schipol Airport: on his flat, peace-loving, self-respecting territory. After the passengers had been released the aircraft had been burned as it stood on the runway. A group calling itself the National Arab Youth Organization had claimed responsibility.

Perhaps in order to demonstrate his new but already developed expertise in his subject Ferrers casually informed me after this first meeting that the NAYO was *only a cover name for the PFLP, the same Marxist-Leninist group which had shot up Athens Airport the previous summer and attempted to assassinate Joseph Sieff on New Year's Eve while he was enthroned on the bog.* He related these facts in a somewhat weary, indifferent manner, as if he were reading out something he had read many times before. This tired tone was of course intended to imply some acknowledgement that this was all just old hat to me: he didn't want to burden me with what he presumed I must already know. I played along. I gave him a suitably sour smile, as if to say: yes, of course I know these things, so why are you bothering to tell me now? As before our meetings in the beech wood I would have to bone up on this new subject in some detail before throwing out crumbs for him to feed on. He continued in the same fixed tone: *training bases in Syria and Lebanon, headquarters in Beirut, financial and operational support from Egypt, Dr George Habash, the group's leader and founder, born in Lydda.* It was his way of ambushing me with his new knowledge, but at the same time he was issuing a challenge, albeit one disguised in self-deprecations.

None of what he had said to me made much sense at the time, except perhaps *Lydda.* I knew two things about Lydda, only two things about Lydda. I knew that on a hot, dusty afternoon in the late summer of 1931 my father had stopped at Lydda on his way down to Jaffa and the coast. He was travelling to England for the first time, to Cambridge, to study Law. And travelling with him was his friend, the Mufti of Jerusalem's favourite nephew, a dark and intense young man with the physique of a prize-fighter and a brilliantined moustache whose uncle had recently escaped from prison and was on the run from the authorities after exhorting his people at the Mosque of Omar to rise up from under the heavy paws of the British lion. It was at Lydda that a messenger from Jerusalem had overtaken the train with a telegram for my father. For a few moments he must have been filled with a terrible apprehension when he saw that a telegram had followed him all the way from Jerusalem in a Model T Ford. But it was just a message from his sister, to say that she was staying at the George V in Paris *and not to miss her on his way to England.* That was the year of the World Fair, when the Eiffel Tower was lit up from the vertex to the base with the giant letters *CITROËN*, and at every street corner there were men selling dirty postcards, and the Champs-Elysées was so thick with prostitutes that a single man could lose his balance and be trampled underfoot.

The only other thing that I knew about Lydda was that three hundred of its inhabitants had been butchered there in a single afternoon. The advancing Haganah forces had arrived in British-armoured scout cars (of which Dinky made excellent scale models), and as they passed they had left dead dogs and donkeys collecting flies in the streets so that the people who had stayed would understand it was now time to leave. This scene would sometimes slip itself into the wake of one of the long battles in the lower gardens. I have no memory of ever learning these details about Lydda, nor of being told these things directly, by my father, or Omer, or anyone else. There is a type of knowledge that seeps into us and which we silently absorb as coral dumbly acquires mazes under the sea.

The week after Ferrers had declared his interest in terrorism I am again sitting at the mahogany table in the headman's dining room. But this time I am there for a Greek lesson. Greek is taught by Mr Furness, a genial octogenarian who comes up from the town especially to take these classes: I never see him in the masters' lodge. Furness likes to remind us he is still a teenager. Like Frederick in *The Pirates of Penzance* he was born on the 29th of February in a leap year. He has used so much Brylcreem over the years that his hair has turned the colour of warm butter. After Fisher, Furness is my favourite master, though I am careful not to let anyone know this.

Occasionally Palgrave or one of the others drops his pen and disappears under the table, braving the kicks, to check a crib, or try to remove someone else's shoe, and then resurfaces at another place around the table. Furness notices everything but pretends to ignore these disturbances. I like to think that they amuse him, and that without them he might soon weary of our turbid readings from *The Iliad*.

Furness is engaged in translating over four thousand

epigrams from something called *The Palatine Anthology*, a collection of Greek verse dating from before the time of Socrates to the end of the Byzantine era, almost two millennia of minor verse. This he refers to as *my labour of Herakles* or *that work which it may not please the Cruel Fates to be completed*. The Fates are cruel, he says, because unlike the other gods they are deaf to the prayers of men. Every week he brings in one of the verses he has been translating: verses on baths, bees, whores, wine, shipwrecks, talking rocks, and all manner of other subjects. He lets us gnaw at the lines for a while, and after we have made a dog's dinner of them he intercedes with his own tidy version.

Today he has brought in some lines for my benefit, an epigram on the earthquake that levelled Berytus in 554 AD. Secretly I feel honoured by this, and I acknowledge this dedication with a weak smile which I hope the others will not notice, though afterwards I will call him an old fart with the rest. He hands round photocopies of the verses:

Ποῦ τελέθει Κύπρις πολιηόχος, ὄφρα νοήσῃ
ἔνδιου εἰδώλων τὴν πρὶν ἔδος Χαρίτων;
τύμβος ἀταρχύτων μερόπων πόλις, ἧς ὑπὸ τέφρην
αἱ Βερόης πολλαὶ κείμεθα χιλιάδες.

Like Fisher he illustrates these handouts with sketches which he calls *parerga*. They are faux-naif in style and intended to amuse us. His hand is unsteady. Perhaps more so than it need be. Today he has sketched some broken columns and dismembered bodies lying among the ruins. These bodies, which could be statues or corpses, are not rendered three-dimensionally. They look like the chalk outlines the police leave behind to show where a body has fallen. After we have each failed to make much sense of the verses he reads out his own translation from his velum notebook; I have the impression that he is picturing something through the

109

lines, but not the scene in question, something from his own life, from the Great War perhaps:

> *Where is Cypris, guardian of the city?*
> *Can she not bear to see the house of the Graces?*
> *That it has become the home of spectres,*
> *A tomb of dead men who had no funeral;*
> *Under whose ashes, we, Beroe's thousands, rest.*

'Not like that today of course, is it, Shadrach? Casinos. Dancing girls. Skiing down the mountains in the morning, and in the afternoon swimming in the Med. That's what they say, isn't it?'

'No, sir. I mean yes, sir.' He is the only master who doesn't mispronounce my name. I am embarrassed by this attention and hope he won't go on. If he addresses me again I resolve to make an insolent reply; otherwise I may pay for it later. But he doesn't, and we open our *Iliads*, duffing back the pages.

I am thinking of that final morning drive along the corniche to the airport. How slowly everything goes by. How slowly everything is moving out in the tinted aquarium of the streets, if it moves at all. There is still so much time, so much time to jump out of the car and disappear.

I have been allowed to ride up front with Omer but my attention is elsewhere. I am clinging to things as they go past. If I can only look at them hard enough they will be more real to me than myself. I will be sucked away into them. I will exchange myself with them. Perhaps, if I concentrate enough, I can steal into the body of the long-haired student already bored in the heat of the morning, sucking on his Fanta by the barricade. How dare he be bored in paradise. When I am being ferried away, spirited out of the city without even a soul noticing. How I envy them their ignorance of me, their leisure not to leave and not to have to go anywhere in a hurry. The men in their white and grey robes, drinking coffee, puffing on hookahs,

110

reading their papers backwards outside the Raoche restaurants. The
fisherman down on the sands, or perhaps he is not even a fisherman,
just a loafer in plastic sandals. The seller of thyme and sesame cakes
on an empty stretch of the corniche, rolling his cart along, calling
Kaik al sumsum kaik al sumsum though there is nobody to hear him
except the gulls and the pigeons. The old men in their keffieh
hunched back to back along the stone mastabah, clicking their worry
beads, shaking their heads. This is the very opposite of an
earthquake. Even the most frail, most abject things survive here,
especially these. And I would change into them too, the weathered
tamarisks which always seem windswept, even on the stillest
mornings, the fly-blown date palms stuck with fading pictures of
Saeb Salam and Piz-Buin sun lotion, the Nido cans and broken
fruit crates that lie beneath the umbrella palms on the edges of the
camps where I will crawl away and vanish.

Then finally, when we are at the airport, there is that fateful
clunk as the boot closes. And I see the old ataal who insists on
carrying all the cases at once, never using a trolley, and beyond the
crazy marble of the terminal floor, and the lonely security man, still
as a telamon in the shade of the uncompleted tourist office. There are
many like him: ordered to guard some spot and then forgotten for
years. All the heralds and harbingers of my homecoming have turned
against me now. Dispassionately they watch me go, perspiring in my
winter clothes.

All winter we have been practising our black-out drills. It has
become impossible to distinguish between the genuine
black-outs and the drills. This may be intentional. During
parades the headman rages against the unions, the commu-
nists, against *fainéant workers*, against *poltroon management*,
against the socialists who he says will abolish private schools
if they are given half a chance. Red stars and hammer-and-
sickles have begun appearing around the school, on the steps

111

up to chapel, on the boards in the refectory, over the photograph of Baden-Powell, in every bog: a graffiti contagion. The Moroccans and Johnny Bunts are assigned to spend their whole day going round with mops and detergents, wiping it all out. Some of the older masters like Magyar and Musson claim yobs are creeping in over-night and putting the filth up, but not even they believe this. Perhaps they are worried that some of the visiting parents will see the slogans. *This is a Fascist Institution. Up the Workers. Through Darkness Light.* Most of these are the work of Standish who is selling typed pamphlets of his own devising entitled *The Wisdom of Mao* and *Our Great Leader Speaks* to juniors at extortionate prices. This is becoming a brisk trade and Sackville has threatened to denounce him unless he is given a fat cut.

Since the black-outs began torches have been coming into their own, spreading their furtive radiance down the long corridors, through the bog-houses and the dormitories. New torch games are evolving. Aldis lamps splutter their messages across the dark rooftops. Obconical beams lighten up the night sky. Nobody is sure what they are looking for, but it is not long before there are sightings, of saucers, of night gliders, of bald eagles. Can birds be blinded, like rabbits, and brought down to earth? It has been discovered that each torch has its own signature-ring pattern when projected on to the ceiling: even those torches of the same model have individual signatures. There are searchlight duels, nightly *son et lumières* of the Battle of Britain, sudden blindings. Some boys lie in wait among the shadows on the stone stairs up to St Cross, torches wedged beneath their chins. As the new men return from the washrooms the place becomes like the tunnel of a ghost train, all the faces lighting up ghoulishly, the torches flickering on and off. When those with heavy-duty torches, the type used in road accidents, hold them against their hands or feet, we see the irradiant

112

corpuscles, the veins, the dim outlines of the skeleton itself; like the aspic flesh of the Abu Brace, scourge of the maids, which flinches from sunlight, from any light, and whose inner workings are clearly visible through its own skin, as though it were a transparent living model of itself. The sight but not the sound of the Abu Brace presages an imminent fatality scored by the hour of its appearance, and the place, and that to which it was contiguous, yet the night patter of the Abu Brace is strangely comforting, statelier than the chameleon, defter than the skittish speckled lizards.

Every night there is the clatter of plastic mugs down the stone stairs. And every morning there are more casualties waiting outside Sister Gab's surgery. Hoping to emerge painted in Mercurochrome. Since the black-outs trip wires have been laid in ever increasing numbers. Many are trapped by those of their own making. Patrol Leaders are preceded by junior decoys who walk a few feet ahead of them down the black corridors, like mine-sweepers.

The Arabs have begun buying London. There are cartoons in the papers of long limousines with a separate door for each yashmaked wife, of camels dropping mounds of steaming dung outside Burlington Arcade, of little men in tea-towels shaking money bags at every British institution: buxom blondes, Stonehenge, stately homes, Nessie; in one sketch some Arabs sucking on cigars are loitering outside Buckingham Palace under an estate agent's sign which reads: *NOT FOR SALE*. Not a day goes by without another story of Arab concupiscence and prodigality being celebrated. And I have become the local gateway to this phantasmagoric Orient, this Araborama. Like one of the fabled tunnels under the school it is essential that this gateway should lead to the unexpected. The era of the

113

Sand Dance, of magic carpets and sheep's eyes, is all but forgotten now. For the first time I am in demand. I have achieved a sort of popularity. But I am the tyrant's chef, and must contrive ever more exotic dishes to satisfy the appetites I have depraved. Only tales of the most barbaric and monstrous opulence will do: nothing short of Vathek and Queen Xenobia. From Mercedes 600s with gold passementerie, from pet panthers with diamond collars, from bespoke opaline 51s, I have graduated to Lear Jets with on-board piranha aquaria, oil tankers customized to accommodate camel races and polo, to the simulacra of Alpine resorts raised up in the wastes of the Rub el-Khald. There was something about a childhood in draughty houses with high ceilings that had created an unnatural craving for such surfeits, such vulgarian utopias. But it was with deep dismay that day after day I saw my inventions surfacing in the papers. I would never be free of them now.

Ferrers had kept his distance from this sheikh fantasia in which I found myself an ever more reluctant ringmaster. He did not go out of his way to condemn my new role however, and sometimes I would notice him squatting on the margins of the circle, pretending not to be listening. Since the ambush in the beech wood (his escape from which Ferrers had never chosen to explain) we had been in the habit of breaking off, separately, from the column of patrols before it dispersed at the lodge. Instead of heading down into the woods, we would double back and rendezvous at constantly shifting points in that square pocket of scrubland which bordered the Sarum Road. At first sight this featureless region of fallen trees covered in ivy, affording little cover, hemmed in on three sides by the drive and the road, seemed more like a trap than a sanctuary. We were hopelessly vulnerable, even to the smallest dragnet of fighters. The place was a mockery of every one of Ferrer's sacred nostrums. Only a novice quarry would hide out in such an area, and for this reason no fighters would bother to look for us here.

Although Palgrave's outward congeniality persisted, intensified even, I had begun to sense a growing emptiness behind his gadfly exterior. His thoughtless interruptions and his coltish enthusiasms concealed their own loss of spontaneity. They were becoming mere mannerisms, a thin but opaque shell. Although he never spoke about the camp, it was rumoured that Palgrave had endeared himself to Duff-Revel in some lasting way. He had begun to rise quickly through the camp hierarchy, from sapper to look-out, and it was even muted that he would soon be initiated as a fighter. It did not go unnoticed that even Sackville had begun to treat Palgrave differently in the dormitory, no longer dispatching him on the more menial tasks.

Palgrave rarely tags along during breaks as he used to, and when he does there is a certain awkwardness, an affectation of togetherness. Everyone knows he spends his break at the fort above the masters' lodge directing the junior Curlews in the construction of an outer ring of earthworks. It has already become apparent to some of those monitoring developments at the fort closely that the works there may never be satisfactorily completed. Although the inner ring of dug-outs and culverts was created almost overnight, and clearly followed some pre-existent plan, the later developments have been ponderous, snagged by mysterious landfalls and collapses. This is a pattern already familiar from the chalk mines in the woods. Carefully canted tunnels are checked by subsidence. Stanchioned underground chambers are discovered the following week to have caved in. It is in the nature of these works never to be completed. Yet, despite Palgrave's growing closeness to the world of the camp, Ferrers continues to speak quite openly in front of him of our plans and ruses. In fact, Ferrers is uncharacteristically voluble when Palgrave is with us. When we are on our own Ferrers tells me that if Palgrave ever betrays us he will break him like a dry twig.

Already I have come to regret ever telling Ferrers about the secret arsenals and shooting-ranges under the refugee camps. If I do not invent new details he goes silent and ignores me for the remainder of the day.

Ferrers' interest in terrorism has become an obsession. He will speak of almost nothing else when we are alone. He keeps a scrapbook. He knows the differences between the PDFLP and the PF-GC, between the ALF and the PNF, between Saiqua and the PFLP. He is fascinated by the shadowy men behind the scenes who are never photographed and whose names are recurrently mis-spelt by the Western press. Men such as Sami Al Attami, the *conductor of Damascus*, secretive master of Saiqua; Dr George Habash, a radical anti-colonialist for whom the eradication of Zionism is merely a skirmish in the epic war against imperialism; Ahmed Jibril, leader of the Palestine Front General Command, a splinter group of the PFLP, the architect of airport massacres and pioneer of suicide bombings, a man so illusive that some have doubted his very existence. For the moment, until I can catch up, I confine myself to correcting his pronunciation, enlightening him on points of local geography and orthography. For the present I am content that he should think I know more than I reveal.

time bomb

Despite the warm tones of the Toulouse-Lautrecs and the pictures of Provence, it is cold in Mademoiselle's classroom. She does not take off her mannish coat with the astrakhan collar, her Hermes scarf. She hops about like old film: poor Mademoiselle, she's all nerves.

She points to the historical map of Europe. 'Metternich say that when France sneezes the rest of Europe catches a cold. What do ee mean?' Palgrave pauses to think of a suitably barbed response. Meanwhile everyone has begun to sneeze, cod French sneezes, in the manner of Inspector Clouseau. *Eauchuuu Eauchuuu*. We laugh so hard the tears run down and stain our notebooks, further solecizing our dictations. Palgrave's considered sally is lost in all the racket.

Like the early explorers of the New World, I had learnt to accept that *here* and *there* were not separate continents but one coextensive land mass. Wherever I go within the precincts of the school I stumble into my house, my garden, my city, that which I would not even notice were I at home. Once I believed that I required the solitude of prayer to summon up my *there*, but now I have begun to see that it is already all around me, reconfigured, as if I were

119

living in a new city built from the masonry of the old. There are concealed entrances leading back, coming out where you least expect them, sudden pits and puzzling realignments, rebuses to the heart. Whenever Cleeve bends over my shoulder a secret door opens and I have stepped back into that dead alley off Bab Idriss where the old Jewish stamp-dealer keeps his shutters down against the sun and cats; or I am paddling in the brackish rock pools beneath the Corniche; or walking in Ain Mreisse on the final day of the khamsin when everything looks as if it has been brought up out of Monsieur S.'s cellars. And when the ring binders on a file catch the light, I am there on the slithery edge watching my father learning how to swim at the club pool, watching how he keeps looking back at the shiny handrails. And when I see the Moroccans in their woolly caps lugging filing cabinets and damaged desks I am back under the West Gate where the *ataals* slump against the breccia wall with the luxurious ease of those who carry heavy weights, keeping their distance from the dumb shoe-blacks and the beggars from the camps, haggling their fares with the wisdom of mullahs. *It may only be a short way, Oustaz, but then it only takes a moment for the soul to depart from the body.*

I rarely see my own face now. There are few mirrors surviving above the chipped enamel sinks in the washrooms, and these seem hardly to be trusted. Occasionally I catch my reflection in the dormitory windows at night. I am beginning to look more and more like Ferrers. His sphinx face is buried beneath mine and gradually it is revealing itself, my own sand features falling away.

Mademoiselle is of indeterminate age. Her plucked eyebrows have been redrawn as indices of mild but perpetual alarm. Her bouffant is too composed, too still, too self-same to be anything but a wig. Whatever the season, the temperature, the humour of the moment, her face remains the undisclosed secret of her chlorotic make-up. Her indeterminacy is ageless.

Standish claims that Mademoiselle was the mistress of a Nazi officer during the war. In our history book *The New Barbarism* there is a photograph of a collaborator with her baby, being escorted by two soldiers, her head shaved, nicked, daubed with lipstick swastikas. She is being jostled and spat on by the angry crowd. I wonder if the crowd know the woman personally, if they have snubbed her in the market for the last five years, or is she just a passing effigy to them, the butt of unexpiated guilts, a propitiatory doll of straw. I hope it is not the former. I try hard not to imagine Mam'selle's exposed pate, shiny and smooth as the dome of the Van der Graff generator.

Mam'selle has told us that she was born in a town in the Lot called Montcuq. We repeat the name fulsomely when-ever possible and she strains repeatedly to be amused by this done-to-death jibe. There are no pictures of the Lot on the walls of her classroom, among the vineyards, the Loire Châteaux and the Toulouse-Lautrecs. And it is impossible to conceive how that moorland fastness of fortified hilltop villages and turreted pigeonniers could have ever given birth to such a delicate oriental figurine.

Our textbook is *Michel Strogoff* by Jules Verne. An odd choice perhaps. (I have my suspicions that French boys of our age are reading *The Count of Monte Cristo*, *The Three Musketeers* or *The Hunchback of Notre-Dame*, of which I already possess bowdlerized editions garnered from the stationers of rue Hamra who stock them for the benefit of the pupils from the Maronite Lycées.) Despite the warm images of France which surround us, we are condemned to wander the wastes of Russia with Michel Strogoff. In fact, the more French we could read the further we travelled from France: Siberia, Guadeloupe, to Atlantis, to the stars. Mam'selle had such elegant, tapering fingers, such inviolate crimson nails, it was difficult to picture her actually tacking up all those bright summertime images herself. Possibly they were the work of one of the Francophile masters, Musson perhaps, who drives down to a little *gîte* near Aix at the end of each summer term.

Whenever, very infrequently, one of Mam'selle's nails (they were real) scratches the blackboard, it is as if we have all been suddenly reprimanded by an invisible screeching bird. Everybody winces, and we wait in silence while she rushes to the window to see if there is any permanent damage. Her writing is like a ball of wool gracefully unravelling, airily, unsnared, pure *Babar*; its gentle loop-the-loops the slipstream of a playful ace soon to dissolve into the sky.

Nobody can make head nor tail of *Michel Strogoff*. We always appear to be starting at different places from where we left off. We spend an entire lesson dissecting a couple of lines, and forget completely what came before. We seem to return to half-familiar paragraphs again and again, while other sections are wholly bypassed. Though it is comparatively short, it is in the nature of this book not to be completed. Even if eventually we reach the end we will never finish it. Nobody knows why Michel Strogoff is wandering across Russia. Is he fleeing, or pursuing, or vainly endeavouring to arrive at a particular destination? Perhaps he just travels for the sake of it, a picaresque pin-ball ricocheting across the wastes in Brownian motion.

As Mam'selle hops about to ward off the cold, the lower hem of her coat with the astrakhan collar flaps open and releases the soft bouquet of naphthalene, which is strange because she rarely wears any other coat. If I arrive late and have to sit in the front row I will smell my mother, and my sister who has begun to use the same fragrance in imitation of the daughter of Monsieur S., and the maids who surreptitiously dab themselves under their arms and between their legs from the bottle on my mother's dressing table; in fact I smell the scent of every woman I know, except Emmy who smells of Chiclets and dried American sweat.

Before Easter we drive as usual to the pine woods above Bhamdoun for the Easter-egg hunt. Emmy has almost finished her cellophaned hoard of eggs by the time we reach the museum crossroads. Her cheeks are blushed with chocolate, her T-shirt draggled in pine needles and more chocolate. With the last rabbit dangling from her lips she has the same glazed and sated expression as Saturn in Fisher's cartoon. The air-conditioning has broken down and my eggs have already melted away into a compound sludge; coloured foil, milk chocolate and dragée, all oozing together. As we pass the museum crossroads I notice that beside the old gendarme in his blue jodhpurs and goggles there is a cluster of soldiers with M16s. Omer slows down as we pass so I can inspect the semi-automatics more closely. The soldiers smile back when they see me staring at their guns. The youngest calls to me. Yella Nimr Yella. All the way home the car is filled with the smell of melting chocolate and with the warm scent of Omer's worry beads.

When we arrive Emmy enlists my help in the search for her Slinky. The search takes us up to the den. The place has undergone some alterations since my last visit. Though the walls are still shades of black, the poster of Iwo Jima with the elliptical peace sign has been replaced by a poster of a scalped skull, with pansies and dandelions growing out of where the lid of the cranium used to be. In the corner by the LPs there is another skull (probably liberated from the Medical School) wearing a black top hat similar to that donned by Baron Samedi, with rooster and pigeon feathers sticking out from the black silk band.

Trench and Judge are occupying separate bean-bags, while Marlin reclines on a divan improvised from a padded deck-chair and Syrian pouffes. A tall hookah has capsized out in the no-man's slough of brimming ashtrays, abandoned graze and crunched-up Fanta cans that lies between Trench and Marlin. A maundering dispute is in progress as to who should reach out and right the hookah. The tenor of this dispute suggests it has been in progress for some time:

'See the last time before last you mussed the B I put it right — right?'

'Yeah but it was my B to muss, grosshead.'

'Yeah like you shit where you eat, man.'

'No fuck — no man owns the B, not even the B man.'

'Whoohoo. Don't like weight me, man. Don't legislate into my head.'

Various appeals are made for us to intervene, but when Emmy recognizes her Slinky she begins to kick Trench with her muddy sneakers and smears chocolate from her hands over his white headband and into his tangled hair. The Slinky, twisted beyond hope, has been put into service as a prosthetic arm, to fetch and ferry pipes, reefers, mugs of Tang, Chupa-Chups, from one recumbent to another, but this present salvage operation is clearly beyond it.

After a while the fallen hookah is abandoned to its fate and all attention turns to Top Cat which has been going throughout. They are all hypnotized by its stylized, diminished world of trash cans, fire hydrants, sloping weatherboards and picket fences. Does it remind them of home perhaps, or does it just remind them of itself. Before the show is finished the soigné newscaster with the wavy hair and affected Maronite accent suddenly comes on. Such abbreviated programming is not uncommon. All three begin to cuss and gob long-distance at the screen. They are accurate, high-calibre gobbers. Their sputum has the requisite ballistic density, true parabolic weighting. Soon the image of the newscaster is receding behind a lanolin of slugs.

After the gobbing has died off Marlin begins coughing. They all begin coughing, calling to each other like dogs in the night. Ratchety, vibrato, old-man tremors, detonating into deep-chest basso quakes. In the middle of all this Trench peers down at his watch, an ancient Timex which he keeps under a sweatband around his ankle. 'Hey, guys. Quinn should be here by now.' The others stop coughing and pay close attention.

'Yeah,' says Marlin, 'the Mighty Quinn.'

Then they all begin chanting together, in a tone of high expectation, as if heralding the arrival of some imminent marvel: 'When Quinn the Eskimo comes, when Quinn the Eskimo, Quinn the ESKIMO comes.'

The man referred to as Quinn is a puny Armenian who I had seen several times being cuffed about by the guards at the West Gate. Among the fruits of Quinn's brief visit is a china pillbox filled with what look like peppercorns. After much cajoling Trench eventually parts with two of these which Marlin and Judge scrutinize minutely between thumb and forefinger before swallowing them down with much grimacing and on-the-spot commentary.

'Yuck-son-of-yuck. Gagtime again . . . Like this is King Grody, man.'

Both Marlin and Judge are pretending to vomit, and they are good at this, doubling up, dangling their tongues down at the sheepskin rug which is covered all over in scraps of silver-foil, as if it were having highlights put in.

'Like. Like bitter is the pill, man.'

'Like Quinn jacked in my fucking mouth.'

'Like summer's coming round again.'

'Kicking. Coming kicking.'

When we return to the den some half-hour later we find Marlin and Trench attempting to bury themselves with a mountain of bean-bags, pouffes and miscellaneous cushions, while Judge cowers in the far corner veiling his head under a Damascene tablecloth. Their condition does not appear to surprise Emmy who promptly sends in her salukis masked in two of last fall's trick-or-treat faces, carbuncled crones with verdigris skin. The salukis galumph about blindly, flattening all the shrines and hookahs and sound equipment which lies in their path, while the boys flee out on to the flat roof, wailing and ululating like Shia women from the south. They have only just begun to recompose themselves when Emmy makes a second foray, entering in that exacting yoga position known as the crab, a scarlet tarboush balanced on her hollow honeydew belly. When they see her the boys abandon the den entirely and run down into the veranda where they shelter behind a rampart of recliners and deck-chairs.

On returning home, after visiting the lower gardens I sit down at my mother's walnut secretary from which the tooled leather has begun to peel with the heat, and fill in my scrapbook for the day. The 14th of April. A bus has been ambushed in the suburb of Ein al-Roumaneh by Phalangist gunmen. At least twenty-seven Palestinians have been killed. This scale of killing is unprecedented in the city. Initially I suspect that the press have commissioned the attack themselves. The local papers are having a feeding frenzy, providing commentary from every party and pundit, delirious eye-witness accounts, photographs of the shot-up bus from many angles, artists' reconstructions of the attack in various phases, pull-out supplements with Kennedy-style diagrams of the trajectories of the assailants' fire. Yet despite all the heated speculation and hypothe-sizing as to the motives behind the attack there is an underlying, paradoxical sense that the event is both entirely surprising and wholly anticipated.

I select and cut out sections from L'Orient, As Safir, and the Herald Tribune, and paste them across two sides of the black album. As I do this I look up to the shelves above my mother's desk. I could recognize the different spines before I could read. Waverley. The Forsyte Saga. The Cherells. The Barchester Chronicles. The spines are covered in the same wilting leather as the desk itself, a distressed orange-brown with still refulgent gold tooling. I look back over the two filled-in sides of my scrapbook, the diagrams, the photographs, and then back to the shelf again. The house is without noise, and the garden, and the campus beyond it. I can hear no traffic down on the corniche, nor distant calls from the lantern-lit caiques pushing out into the dusk. Casually at first, then metronomically, then in panic, my eyes move between the scrapbook and the shelf, groping for a reconciliation that will not come.

Later, crouching among the carob trees, watching my parents as they walk down to the Plymouth, I can be reconciled at least to the disconnectedness of things, and to the indifference between them.

So the summer term took its uncertain course. After a school trip to Versailles, a craze for bangers swept through the school, followed by a craze for starting fires with magnifying glasses. When the lower pavilion, used to store the high-jump pallets, was burned to the ground, ushering in a new season of punishment parades, Standish was ready to cash in, having secretly stockpiled quantities of miniature ball-in-the-hole puzzles and Rubik's cubes.

On the shortest night of the year Palgrave was found buried alive in one of the inner chambers of the chalk mines: it took five hours to dig him free.

Furness suffered a stroke while cutting his wisterias but returned after only three weeks away flourishing a series of Byzantine epigrams on paralysis.[2]

Ferrers' obsession with terrorism did not relent, not even for a day. His scrapbook bulged with accounts of aborted hijackings, murderous attacks on school buses, Katyusha bombardments of Northern Galilee. Sometimes at night I would dream of the blood seeping out from between the pages and trickling down the stone stairs and shutting the eyes of winking mica. Everyone was surprised when Ferrers came forward and confessed to painting swastikas on the posters in Mam'selle's classroom. It was only the thoroughness of his reports to the Correspondent Society which saved him from expulsion.

[2] I have been able to trace only one: 597, Book IX, *The Palatine Anthology*, 'Εν 'Ανάξαρβῳ, attributed to Cometas Scholasticus, which begins: *I have been paralysed to the soles of my feet, halfway between life and death, near to Hades, breathing, but otherwise an utter corpse . . .*

I am aware that this brief gazette of the term differs in some particulars from that published in *Boreas*, the official chronicle of life at North Hill. This must reflect my increasingly lopsided view on all that was evolving in the shallow spaces around me that summer.

On the day that school broke up for the term I was to take the train to Yorkshire, to be billeted on my long-suffering grandmother. I had not seen Ferrers throughout the morning and would not have been especially surprised to learn that he had already slipped away without saying goodbye, yet I had the sense that he was still there somewhere within the school. Although inconspicuous when present, there was something about Ferrers' proximate absence which communicated itself through the pace in the corridors, through the expression on passing faces and in the aspect of empty classrooms. I remember I looked for him first in all the usual places: the pavilion, the trunk room, the practice cubicles in the Music School. Eventually I found him in the upper gardens, squatting on the bank of the lily pond. He was looking intently across at the war memorial on the other side. Sometimes in the winter when the pond froze over juniors would come here and roll Dinky cars and trucks across the ice. These would often fall through, and when the better weather came for a week or two you would see boys fishing from the bank for sunken treasures. But after the brief fishing season this part of the garden was rarely used.

His Gladstone bag sat on the mossy ground beside him. He was clutching his scrapbook in both his arms. It had grown into two volumes which he had stuck together, as one sticks two passports together, the old still containing valid visas. The memorial itself was surmounted by a bronze statuette of a naked boy holding up his right hand to the sky, and on the pigeon-stained base were inscribed the words: *Here am I, send me.* Ferrers continued to stare across the still dark water and the floating islands of the lily leaves. If he had noticed me behind him he did not let on. I left him there and walked back towards the school which was almost quiet now. Most of the cars had gone from the front drive. I made my way past the few stragglers still waiting apprehensively at the front of the drive, and headed down the Sarum Road. Past the garden centre, the hospital, past the prison, towards the station. And all the time I knew Ferrers was still sitting where I had left him, as motionless as the monument he protected.

Interlude

David was scanning the embankment and the signs, his shoulders hunching up again. He was determined not to miss the turning.

When he was sure he had found it we left the road we no longer recognized and joined a tailback leading down to a large lit-up roundabout beside a shopping centre. David began to whistle to himself, the song which had just been on the radio, softly. Then he realized what he was doing and stopped.

'Rush hour in the country too these days.' He gestured out at the line of winking back-lights below.

'Could be an accident.'

'Not around here.' He began whistling again, a little self-consciously this time; it was one of the tunes he used to practise on his cello up in the playroom at the top of the house before it was a playroom. A gigue by Bach. Despite the oncoming lorries he whistled well, but without much expression; and after he had stopped the tune continued to play through my head, doubling back over itself, cyclical but sterile.

The old ring-road had all but disappeared now. But we could clearly see the new motorway's necklaces of light running round through the hills beyond the water-meadows and down towards the coast. In silence we stared at all those distantly diminishing lights as the traffic ahead of us crawled slowly down to the roundabout.

'That's really why they protest, I suppose . . . because it's beautiful. And useful too.' As David spoke I picked up a velvet-covered barrette from the console and began to twist it in my fingers.

'And how's Rachel?'

'Oh the same. The same.' The thing was beginning to bend in my fingers. My teeth ground pleasantly together as silently I broke it.

'And the quangos, the advisory committees on fair trading?'

'You've already asked me all that.'

'Of course I have.'

David had relaxed again now that he was certain he knew the road. He kept looking out of the window and rubbing his bloodshot almond eyes, not that there was anything much to see quite yet, just more cars, empty pavements, some women carrying shopping bags across a footbridge. He had stopped following the signs. As we slowed again he began peering between the hoardings, trying to catch the squat tower of the cathedral perhaps, or maybe just something he could recognize.

Part Two

orientals at heart

The unseasonable warmth had fooled the daffodils and narcissi along the lower banks. We criss-crossed through them, our jackets slung over our shoulders, Palgrave absent-mindedly trampling on the flowers as we passed. We had all grown suddenly taller now that so many of the seniors had gone, though nothing had quite prepared us for the feeling of it, like a sudden change in air pressure. We were lightheaded but lost too in a way. It was difficult to get our bearings right, now that so much had gone.

'There's no need to hide, no one to run from any more.' This was Palgrave's new refrain, his universal condiment for the silences which fell ever more often between us. He had picked up a small divining twig from the dewy grass which he began twitching in the direction of the Sarum Road. While Ferrers was looking back at the tracks of deeper greenness running down through the trampled flowers, down from the higher banks under the great spreading horse-chestnuts.

'And how do you know for sure, dungbrain?' Ferrers spoke without turning round.

'But not now the Duffer's left.'

'And what if he's still hiding out somewhere? Or gone to join the horse, down in the woods?'

Within a few weeks discipline at the camp had begun to break down. With no chambers and passages collapsing there was little work to do, and the will was lacking to begin any new tunnels. Desertion had become increasingly commonplace until there were so many quarries in the woods that they began to outnumber the remaining fighters and mount raids on the camp itself. The camp was all but abandoned now. The earthworks at the fort above the masters' lodge had also ground to a halt for lack of workers. With the command structure weakened by repeated coups and rebellions the works had fragmented into several independent pockets; the interconnecting passages and trenches had been left to become a boggy wasteground where juniors now played unhindered.

Although raids continued between the dormitories, the new generation of patrol leaders had taken to more courtly forms of rivalry. Savage, Sackville's successor, and Bass, the new leader of the Curlews, had begun to visit each other in caparisoned chariots constructed from rugs and padded with pillows against splinters; these chariots were drawn by teams of juniors and accompanied by retinues of fan-wallahs and praetorian guards bearing staves and towel balls. Lighter fighting chariots had also evolved. These provided sport for the new leaders who would watch their champions from a high dais of mattresses replete with fine refreshments, quippers and masseurs. Betting on the chariots was heavy. A new breed of bookies with Standish at their head had replaced the old protected brokers. The fashion for delicate consumables had pushed down the value of the old durables. I had seen whole arsenals of sheath knives and catapults

being wagered against one slim ice-blue box of *Chabonnel &
Walker*. Some would lose all they had fought for over the
years in a single brief fight.

Ferrers was too heavy for the fighting chariots and had
nothing of value left to bet with. While the fights were
raging out in the corridor he would sit in the empty
dormitory beside his bed reading books which he later
hid in the the trunk room. Before he used to keep his
distance from the others, but nobody had really noticed.
Now everyone left him alone. Even Palgrave, who always
used to make a point of engaging Ferrers in weightless
conversations, had begun to leave him alone.

Slowly at first, but now with the force of a routine, chess
and trictrac have begun to flower in every dormitory. It is a
sign of how much has changed. Nobody had the leisure or
the liberty for such things before. On the nights without
chariots everybody is huddled in small groups around the
edges of the dormitory as if around camp fires. The betting is
more moderate than on the chariots as match results are
more predictable. Everyone has become accustomed to
setting up the pieces from memory after raids. The lost
pieces are replaced by Subuteo men, conkers, pebbles,
Belgian chocolates in their matt foil wrappings. Most of
the prize boxes of chocolate must be stale by now, but this
does not appear to affect their trading value. Only the patrol
leaders and their favourites are ever seen to eat them anyway.

Nobody seemed particularly surprised when Girl and Cooke
began playing music in the dormitory. Cooke had suddenly
produced a small gramophone shaped like a briefcase with
the speaker in the lid. Then after half-term Girl brought
back a shiny red Sony cassette-recorder, with a little handle
so that he could take it about with him wherever he went.
At first when I noticed they were both wearing the same
type of strange boot I assumed this must be a coincidence.

They were ankle-boots, snub-nosed with chunky heels and purple silk lining. I had never seen anything so ugly. Sometimes Girl and Cooke would try to play the same song at the same time on both their machines, so they could hear it in stereo. Inevitably one machine lagged behind the other; this gap would widen as the performance continued until it became an echo, a dialogue of parrots. It vexed me greatly that I could not know if the seemingly senseless words of the songs they played represented encrypted clues to some distant and forbidden universe, or were simply random gibberish to fill in the tunes. *Coo-Coo-Ca-Goo. CheepaCheepa CheepCheep. Monkey got broke and we all went to heaven in a big glass boat.* Sometimes they would dance and clap and mouth the words when the songs were playing loud. It made me sick watching them, and I was pleased to see that it was all getting under the skins of Barnsley and Ferrers too. One evening when we were at a loose end we went over and gave them both a good kicking; they were too wet to fight for each other so we dealt with them each in turn. The next morning during break I saw Cooke paying juniors to run the gauntlet of the drive outside the head-man's study to search the thickets for all the ejected cassettes and singles.

On his last day, at the end of the summer term, Duff-Revel had sent a couple of his Curlew lackeys to bring me in. At first sight it had looked as if the fort was deserted. All the workers and the fighters have gone. Although it is a dull day and they do not catch the light I notice the convoluted pipes of the old gasworks beyond the boundary fence, and I think I will run there if things get bad. They lead me to the central dug-out which is lined with transparent polythene and the remains of some desks. Duff-Revel is down there on his own, squatting on the ground though there is a chair of sorts beside him. When I am down in the dug-out he gestures for the other two to go. He has been drinking one of the headman's bottles of Cyprus sherry and there are some packets of the headman's Players on the ground about him. He mashes these into the duckboard with his out-stretched heel. I realise it is the first time that I have been really close up to Duff-Revel in all the years I have been at the school. Even this close there remains something loose and unfocused about the face. Perhaps I have become too used to seeing it always at a distance, across the drive down to the woods, on the far side of a dormitory, through the netting of the tennis court. It does not occur to me for a moment that this might be the last I see of him. For some reason I cannot bear to look into his slack jaw and bottle eyes. It spooks me and I know then that the only way I will save myself is to think of his topspin forehand down the line: the balance and the totality of it somehow bear me up to face him without cringing.

Ferrers had been Duff-Revel's man in the dormitory, and Duff-Revel's man in the woods. After he had told me he did not wait to see my reaction. He looked up into the dull sky, and I knew he wanted me to leave at once. The raid in my first term, the disappearance of the staves in the woods, my betrayal at the crater: these had never seemed mysteries, but the revelation itself was a mystery of sorts, a final poisoned valediction, the effects of which Duff-Revel knew he would never enjoy. Leaving was a sort of death for him, I think, and the dying must seek consolation in such mischief.

Never had Ferrers appeared more admirable than he did now. I envied Ferrers his long cunning and I wished ardently to protect him from ever knowing he had been found out. And particularly at this time when his isolation made him want to conceal his continuing obsession from me, an obsession which he could share with no one else. There

143

were no signs of the scrapbook any more. This worried me beyond measure. My own black-paged scrapbook functioned as a necessary burial ground. Persons and events were entered with due obsequies and then forgotten. I rarely looked back at anything. Even a two-page spread like the Ein al-Roumaneh massacre would have lain undisturbed for many years had it not borne such monsters. But though Ferrers had seemed to abandon his scrapbooks I sensed that he continued to cut and paste invisibly, scoring all the killings and counter-killings and bombings and failed bombings into the black pages of his memory. His approaches had become shyer too, as if he had finally become embarrassed by himself. Often he pretends not to want to listen. Rather than bartering lore and know-how, as he used to, he proceeds by indirection and obliquity. He asks what he already knows the answer to so that I may expand on some adjacent matter. He makes deliberate gaffes in the hope that I will overcorrect him.

There is only one school trip a year, and we are senior enough now to go to the Southsea funfair instead of Chesil Sands which are a deadly bore. At first I do not recognize the two young matrons who have come without their white smocks. They are sitting beside Cleeve, and the driver keeps offering them cigarettes which they refuse, tittering a little. Cleeve, who has kept his tweed suit on despite the heat coming through the convex magnifying-glass windows, has said nothing all the way down but now we have arrived he announces that we will have to go past the house where Kipling was locked up in the cellar before we can disembark at the funfair. He begins to issue directions to the driver. We trundle up and down the narrow streets between the low terraced houses but we cannot find the turning to the sea. All

144

the time the driver is becoming more bolshy and we are all hoping he will blow his top at Cleeve, but he just keeps muttering to himself and shaking his head. Perhaps he doesn't want to make a bad impression on the matrons. When we have gone down what appears to be the same terraced street for the umpteenth time Palgrave pipes up at the back, some nonsense about exceedingly good cakes, and Cleeve comes all the way down the aisle and gives him such a cuffing that his bow tie completely unravels and he misses the way again putting it back together.

In the end there is not enough time to stop. It is one of the larger houses near the seafront but I am not certain which. All the houses that have not been converted into hotels with fairy lights and glad-rag paint schemes have the same sullen and undistinguished façades. There is something wretched about this bottom coast. As if all the abject things, the dregs, had gradually slipped down and collected here, unable to sink any further.

After the charabanc stops I notice that Ferrers does not go into the fairground with the rest but slinks off down to the beach. I follow him, but once I am below the level of the promenade I cannot see him anywhere so I begin to trudge back over the grey and stony sand towards the arcades and what I assume must be the Wild Mouse which doesn't look nearly as high as I expected it would.

The week before I left Omer had taken me to a quiet stretch of the beach, near where we used to have the wooden beach house before it was carried away by a storm. My father had said only a fool would build it again in the same place, and all that was left of it now was some wooden struts on which the floorboards used to stand. We'd never used the place much anyway. From where we had come out on the beach I could see right down along the shore to the Pigeon Rocks, and the giant Ferris wheel beyond them. Omer had stood behind me and steadied my skittish shoulders. I held on to the automatic with both my hands, so tightly it hurt. The nozzle was discoloured,

145

though not rusty exactly, and there was dirty tape around the bottom of the handle where the rounds went in. Whenever I had imagined handling weapons in the lower gardens they had been mint and greased, but this had that special feel of things that haven't been touched for a long time: cold, and antique almost, like I imagined one of the trophies on the wall in Milton would feel. Omer said it was called a Todarev 7.62, though there was no name or number inscribed on any of its visible surfaces. 'Mittl Browning Mittl Browning,' he kept telling me, as if somehow that made it all right.

Omer had explained that every target I selected was perched on an invisible vertical line. I had to draw the gun up the groove of that line with both my hands until the sight bars were aligned. 'Squeeze the trigger as if it were your lover's most tender place,' he whispered behind me. When I fired there was a terrible rending of the air. I thought the thing would fly out of my hands high into the sky, but the second time I was expecting it, and after that I wanted to believe that the gulls I was aiming at were diving down into the sea with my bullets in their fat breasts.

I lower my arms and walk on towards the arcades. Somewhere behind the shut-up kiosks and windlass housings further down the beach Ferrers is watching. Unlike most he has a way of putting his spied-upon at their ease, of scrambling their radar, guaranteeing their privacy. Over the previous months I have sensed that he has often been observing me unseen, though of course this is impossible to verify, and I have felt vaguely flattered, but also a touch unsettled, for it proves that ultimately he wants more than this simple companionship of intelligence sharing and discreet mischief.

Just inside the entrance to the funfair there is a hapless mix of Curlews, Hounds and Stags, carrying their Burberrys because of the heat. This is the lot that have spent their money too quickly or are already owned by Standish and the other bookies. The patrol leaders and their favourites are further in, ragging on the dodgems and the centrifuge and the twister which the champions have to ride no-hands while Bass and his quippers look on from below. Though this is against the rules the youths running the rides let them continue. Bass has probably paid up for this priviledge in advance. There is no Ferris wheel here. The highest point is the far loop of the Wild Mouse where it runs out without supports, sheer, over the sea. I pay my 5p, and without waiting for more passengers the small pink capsule rattles off up the ramp. As it rounds the high exposed loop the ride grates and stalls. This must be a deliberate effect. I turn to get a view of the beach below, hoping I will catch Ferrers emerging from his hiding place. But all I see is the blank continuum of grey sky and grey sea. Then I am shooting downwards through the keen air. I am seven-sixty-two millimetres in diameter. Piercing through the rainbow breasts of pigeons which coo forlornly in the mornings. I go round and round without getting out of the pink capsule until all my money is used up.

The ground is heaving all the way over to the coach, as if I had just come ashore. Ferrers is already right at the back, and he has saved a place for me.

When we return I lie in bed and cannot remember the last time I saw Omer and I know I will not sleep until I do. Whenever I try to picture him I see only a silly scene in the Plymouth the day before my sister left to go to live in London. *We are driving fast along the flooded corniche, splashing past the Raoche cafés. My sister is sitting up front and Omer is wearing his peaked green cap in her honour and I am squeezed in on the back seat with all the old clothes and toys she has brought to hand out at the camp before she leaves. But at the entrance a Fatah official with a Palestinian flag on the arm of his green fatigues comes over to tell us we cannot go any further. The camp is completely flooded.*

147

Women are wading across the sandy mud on either side of the car carrying sodden rugs and blankets to dry on the flat roof of the sentry house. We wait inside the car as Omer pulls out all the boxes and lugs them across to the sentry house. Some of the brightly coloured clothes spill out into the mud.

We sit and argue about the seating arrangements for the journey home while Omer goes down to visit his father and little sister Farida who live in one of the hollows below the entrance until the windows steam over and we can no longer see anything outside. When I rub away some of the moisture and peer out I see Omer standing with the official in the mud counting out some dollar bills. But this was not the last time I had seen him, nor even the time before that, and it did me no good to remember it.

green line

Under my grandmother's land rich seams of coal join but her diminished estate is built upon the calcined bones of long-extinct animals which leaven the clay down in the valleys. The museum stillness of her rooms reproaches all but the stealthiest movement, as do the samples which must only be dusted with feathers, or blown with dry breath *to avoid condensing the colourings*; when she does this Mrs Sutcliffe pouts like an old coquette.

There is nothing remotely casual or reticent about the deploying of all these samples from the other potteries, especially not the grander ones. The stoneware Minton cherubs and Dickens characters by Ridgeways stand sentry duty on the shelving in the hall so that even the dropper-in will heed them. On either side the Wedgwood plaques of ladies grieving over urns are brought into perspective by humbler Castleford pastoral scenes, and beyond, the Rockingham chinoiserie in defiantly unoriental file masses to overwhelm the incipient guest. Though it's principally Father George and the family who call these days, and their visits are becoming fewer and more far between.

My grandmother has been poorly as long as I can

remember but since my last visit her eyes have grown that kohled blackness of old women in the souk. At the time I thought this might be the result of too much looking in. She watches *Crossroads* and *Coronation Street* back to back, and then anything except the news, preferably comedy shows when she laughs merrily along and then flinches from the pain inside herself. I pretend not to see this and laugh as well though I do not understand any of the jokes. During the day she siffles up the previous night's jingles while she works on an enormous jigsaw puzzle of a Constable with tiny pieces which are all the same shape, and in the same muffled browns and greens. She constructs the jigsaw on the livid-green card table. It is a matter of honour that she will not venture a piece unless she is certain it will fit. It amuses her that I am so hopeless at selecting the right ones, and when I try to jam down pieces that won't quite go in she regards me contemptuously, but at the same time a little indulgently, as if I were some novice hooligan trying to mess with the great chain of Being. While we play I try not to look at the guttering-out in her still keen eyes.

During the day I pretend to go for long walks but stay quite close to the house. The drive comes out on to what is known as the Tadcaster Road (though this road leads also to Wetherby, Harrogate and Leeds) which I follow down to the church and back, walking through the long grass verges to avoid the spray from the brewery lorries; family lore has it that after only a few minutes in Tadcaster the reek of the hops will send the unaccustomed all squiffy. I try to walk the whole way without looking up, as Father George does. There's not much to see anyway. Just the viscous puddles along the roadside which have the same iridescent gloss as the kipper oil on those mornings when the sun shines through the high windows of the refectory. For a moment I almost want to be back at North Hill, but before it can take root I excise this obscene thought and bury it away with all the other unadmitted wishes.

Those beds and rockeries in view of the main windows have still been kept up, but beyond the garden falls away into rankness and untended lawns. The tiger-lily pond which only a few summers ago had teemed with quivering fish has dried into a black slough. Only the vegetable garden has been saved though it is difficult to recognize what is growing there now. Yet, despite their sadness, the gardens still exert their strange attraction, drawing me down to what has always been euphemistically known as the tennis court. This rectangular wilderness has changed the least of course. Nature has been gardener here time enough to establish her own profuse order. The wire-netting that once bordered the court has become a trellis for weeds and self-sown creepers, and blistering shale has long given way to moss and dark shadows where frogs mooch and parley. Somewhere at home there is a photograph of my mother when young playing here in a white pleated skirt and a hair-band. She is only about Emmy's age and can't be much of a player but she holds the racket confidently enough, scooping her backhand as the ladies did in those days. Once when she had seen me looking she said *That was still wartime, I believe*, and I remember going over and over the picture for some trace of the war, but finding nothing there, not even the faintest hint of a fighter in the colourless sky.

Every night there is a different steaming pudding. My grandmother supervises their preparation during the afternoons. There is Bread and Butter Pudding, Suet, Queen of Puddings, Lemon Pudding, Spotted Dog, and at the weekend Rhubarb Crumble, made with best Wakefield rhubarb. Some of the afters served in the refectory also bear the same hallowed pudding names but all resemblance ends there. For

153

lack of anything else to say I remark on this every evening to my grandmother, and she smiles back at me knowingly, and just as I am about to ask if I can get up she whispers *But that's only as it should be.*

After dinner I quickly retire to my room which is cluttered with mildewed hat-boxes, mostly empty, and puffy eiderdowns. I look down on to the first completed house on the new estate which is being built for Leeds commuters where the old paddock used to be. With my grandmother's opera glasses which I have discovered among the boxes I can watch *The Nine O'Clock News* through their as yet uncurtained french windows. Every night they show the same footage of boys firing down from the shells of the Holiday Inn and the Phoenicia towards Jounieh. I recognize a couple of them from the barricades. They spray out their bullets as if they were hosing down a car. I know I will be granted a glimpse of Omer before the half-term is up. In a city of bad shots he is one of the elect who has the knack of firing an AK47 straight, and his skills will not go unwitnessed. But what I fear most is that the war will be over and I will have missed his glorious transfiguration, though even if the worst happens I will insist that I saw everything when I return. Already the Palestinians and Mourabitoun are scaling the eastern flanks of Sanine to flush out the Maronites from Uyun Al-Siman and Aintura. At night I am kept awake by the thought of all those millions who will see Omer and yet not recognize him. And only the knowledge that Ferrers will be among those millions can soothe away the horrible waste of it.

The day after I returned Cleeve invited me into the stationery room, more of a large cupboard really off the lower corridor. Once the door has been closed nobody will

open it
about this,
every lock in
only means of p...
room, or if there is ...
back against the door. ...
the Spearmint. I try not
difficult in such a confined sp...
he is pushing about the pages
habit, I suppose. The door is so th...
whisper, but still he lowers his voice.

'I'm sorry that you've not been paying
this term, Shady.' He knows of course that I a... ...e
who ever does, although naturally I try to disg... ... He
must want to shake any complacency out of me. I did not
protest. *And I was sorry that the Kipling house did not interest
you.* I thought of the many virgin dividers and compasses
waiting patiently in their tin-box silos on the shelves. All that
sleeping potential to scratch and inscribe and deface. I was
comforted by the thought of it all so close to me at that
moment, as I was when in the darkness I pictured the mint
armouries sleeping under the camps. I had realized now that
Cleeve was not wishing to make sense.

It is strange being hit in the dark. You do not know when
the next blow will come, and the blows fall in odd places
because the hitter cannot see properly what it is he is doing.
And Cleeve was a poor hitter even in the light. Now he
came at me with an open but slightly cupped hand. Instead
of drawing back for a proper swing he let his hands remain
for a moment wherever they fell, suckering blindly at my
neck and my throat. It was as though he feared having
nothing to hold in the darkness. His hands betray him. They
whisper his true nature into my flesh, and at that moment I
want nothing more than to thank them for their tender
confidences by disinterring Omer's corroding gift from the

glinting round into his
ps sensing something of this
hit me more forcefully again, and
y, his eyes having adjusted to the light. Only
e heard me beginning to blub did he stop and wait,
clearing his throat before opening the door and then
shutting quickly behind him, leaving me alone in the
darkness which I was thankful for.

More than anything else I feared my face would be
stained in some indelible way by the blubbing. I ran the
back route round to the changing rooms and rubbed hard
under my eyes with a muddy games towel. All the mirrors
were broken or gone so I still could not tell if any traces
remained. Upstairs in the dormitory everybody was
crouching around the helix-shaped race track which
Standish had brought back from half-term. The betting
was heavy and reckless, as it always was after a holiday,
though the set was almost certainly rigged in some way.
There were reports that even the chariot fights were being
fixed now. Someone had already lifted the opera glasses
which I had stowed temporarily under the Vyella shirts in
my chest. I should have known better than to leave them
so exposed. Some Stag or Curlew bookie would have them
by now, though Palgrave insisted he had seen Cooke
watching the track through them only a few minutes
before. I went over to question Cooke but he denied it
vehemently, claiming he had just seen Palgrave demonstrating their uses to a group of junior Curlews in the
washrooms. When I put this to Palgrave he pranced off to
confront Cooke waving a sock-ball, and no sooner had
they begun to scramble on the floor than they were
surrounded by a fast-growing circle of punters waving
long boxes of Bendick's and thin bars of Lindt. Standish
stood on the chest above them holding a small blackboard
on which he chalked up the shifting odds.

I found Ferrers in the trunk room with one of the old *clobber sticks* which nobody wanted much any more; the trunks had formerly been used for defensive palisades and tormenting claustrophobics but now they remained more or less undisturbed. He had brought up a stack of books from the history room which fell open at the pages with grisly photographs. Skeletons sitting in the trenches still in their greatcoats. A beheading in Mandarin China. Bulldozers pushing away the thin dead of Dachau. He had been looking at a volume on the rise of the Nazis, but he pushed it in among the other books when I came in, as if I had caught him reading something dirty which he was afraid I might spread around. That night I dreamt I had opened a history of the war at the photograph of my mother scooping her backhand. Palgrave and the others crowded round, as they always did when someone had found a good picture in one of the books, and I had felt foolish, and refused to admit that I did not understand why the photograph had been included.

Upstairs the house smells wistfully of coal dust and lavender talc, of better days. That evening I did not touch the phrenological head which stands outside my little room, as I had done whenever I had entered for as long as I could remember. I climbed up on the deep attic sill with the opera glasses and focused in. But that night they had installed their new curtains and there was nothing to see through the french windows except the outlines of the occupants crossing like fish in a dirty bowl. I kept watching in the hope that the curtains might part again, but they did not. I know that it was on this night that Omer appeared in glory to the world. Though they would not have recognized him I am certain that no one could have failed to distinguish him

157

from those others on the bullet-frayed ledge smoking between exchanges with their cans of Coca-Cola. Even those who do not know what they are watching will find they are not able to pry away his burning image from their dreams.

the brotherhood

And the war had made me rich. There was fierce demand for the 7mm. and the 9mm. strays which I had harvested from the kitchen garden, as there was for the cartridges and other trophies with which Mona and Lamia returned each week having picked their way back from the southern suburbs. The cartridge shells were particularly prized as they could be used as whistles, converted into necklaces, or affixed to webbing adapted from snake belts. Standish had invested all his takings from the previous term in Swiss liqueurs and truffles and Patum Peperium only to find that the action had moved on. Now military durables were the thing and Standish had caught a heavy cold. For the first time we were witness to the strange spectacle of juniors scoffing themselves on what had hitherto been the exclusive fare of patrol leaders and their favourites. Within days the sickbay was overflowing with the runs. It was evident that the junior stomach did not adjust peaceably to the diet of sybarites and courtesans.

I was fortunate in being in a position to control the supply of rounds, cartridges and shrapnel, and could therefore ensure that trading values remained relatively steady. Attempts by competitors to broaden the market with military memorabilia, medals, war postcards, flasks, belt-clips, and the like, had so far largely failed. But without the patronage of Savage and Bass and their courtiers I would have been nothing. The nightly spectacle of the leaders reclining on their dais festooned with bandoliers of cartridges, casting shrapnel at the feet of the bookies, regaling their champions with snub-nosed 9mm.s and dum-dums, afforded the most comprehensive and influential endorsement I might have ever wished for. However, though I probably now had the wherewithal to run my own chariot team and retain the services of manicurists, masseurs and jesters, I heeded Ferrers' advice and forsook the ways of the dais. Certainly it had not been the vagaries of the market alone that had brought Standish low. Once he had purchased for himself all the fine privileges of a courtier and now he was knocking out Trebors in the washrooms.

It was late May, or possibly already June: in any case the old bog-houses had begun to smell, and this was a sure harbinger of summer, though the smell would be lost on us in a day or two. Ferrers and Palgrave and I were standing at ease and faces to the wall outside the headman's study, waiting to be beaten. The previous night some Buffaloes had climbed into the garden centre along the Sarum Road and heisted several smoke bombs designed for flushing out moles; these had been set off in Milton during the morning parade to no little effect. For reasons that remained unclear we had been blamed. In such circumstances it paid not to complain.

'Think how many times some saps have taken the can for what we've done.' Ferrers flicked a glob of snot at Palgrave which landed on his cheek, and then Palgrave flicked it away at the portrait of the founder.

'But better that one innocent be set free than ten guilty punished.' Palgrave did not look up from his wall as he spoke.

162

'Better for wets and nicksters you mean.' It was not usual for Ferrers to be so talkative.

'And low-lifers and con-artistes and privateers.'

The two of them began giggling into their handkerchiefs, like horses with nosebags, until Magyar passed by and gave them both a shut-it kick. After Magyar had gone Palgrave started murmuring jokes which I couldn't hear properly, and Ferrers continued to laugh along. Occasionally I would make out words like *light bulb* and *Irishman* and *shark*. The shelves of Palgrave's joke godown were heavily stocked with such material. He shifted it to all comers and in all weathers. But Ferrers was really going for it, hunching up his shoulders and shaking like an old woman. His face went all to pieces when he giggled. I suspected my face also did this, when I giggled and tried to hold it back at the same time. I turned away. I could not bear to watch him any longer.

I had stood in that same spot enough times to understand what it offered in the line of visual distraction, and that wasn't a whole lot. This wall was not unlike that sort of acquaintance with whose presence one is utterly familiar, but on whom one never bestows the least consideration once one is out of their company. This type of local knowledge was possessed by not a few of our number, yet it could never be shared or acknowledged. Among the wall's chief attractions were the photographs of dead old boys. Though they wore the same cricket jerseys, the same blazers and caps, they were a different race entirely: unused to cameras they held themselves stonily, their awkward bearing and defensive eyes betraying little except perhaps an almost Mediterranean sense of their own honour. It was the same look, of being pledged to what will not be read, that I had seen in the eyes of the young Maronite men who were at that moment holed up under fire on the cold slopes of Sanine. Musson would sometimes tarry by this same section of the wall to point out

163

the future leader of the British Fascist Party who posed in full costume among the cast of *L'Avare* before a summer performance in the woods; it was not clear from the picture which role he had been given. There, in the row below, was another unfortunate future man of the right, the son of a Liberal cabinet minister who would go on to fight with Franco and carouse his way around wartime Berlin with his French mistress, instructing all his unpaid bills to be forwarded directly to the Führer's private office. Nothing in his life became him quite like the leaving of it, and he met his end in Wandsworth prison joking lightly with the prison chaplain and thanking the warders for their unflagging hospitality. And yet he was the only one in the picture whose eyes were not closed while being open: he sports a long white silk scarf and already he wears the airs of a practised dandy.

It was only when I faced the wall that I saw the porn. It never came to me during the night, nor during the doldrum lows of classes, but there it remained tethered to that stretch of wall where it waited for my inevitable return . . . *I had gone with Emmy to visit my father's office. The student occupation had just ended and the barricades had all come down. There were Squad 16 men in dark glasses lining the wrecked atrium and the veined marble stairs. My father had lagged behind to congratulate them on a job well done and hand round packets of Marlboros. Emmy ran ahead and began spinning herself round and round in one of the high-backed conference chairs, fanning the still, hot air. It was evident from the first that none of the original 51s would have survived. Every surface in the room was littered with mouldering sandwiches, old newspapers, cans, and there were cigarette butts stubbed out into the furnishings. The curtains had been ripped down and used as blankets over a makeshift bed of uprooted leather cushions from the conference chairs. Despite the desolation, I decided to make a thorough check, and started working through the drawers and the filing cabinets. I found the thing rolled up in the makeshift* bed; it was tallowy, and twisted at both ends like a cracker. Inside it was all giant breasts. There must have been faces too but I don't remember them. Some were swollen and distended like the bellies of starving children. Others were long and pendulous, as if they had been weighted down for years. And there was one pair that were creased and gone like defunct balloons. This was nothing like the girly magazines at the airport and the bookshops along rue Hamra where the models on the covers were as proud and erect as the girls on the billboards outside the casinos and revues of Jounieh. No, these breasts were misshapen clowns begging to amuse. It was pitiless and spiteful to overlook them. The court dwarf reminds the courtiers that Nature is nothing but a vain freak, and if all nature is a freak then each part and portion must be vouchsafed an equal dignity.

And later that same sweltering afternoon we had returned through the close streets of Ain Mreisse where everything was as it always had been, only slower, much slower, and when we came to the villa there was shouting and crashing up on the top floor instead of slow music and silence and of course without waiting we ran together up the cool white steps to see what it was about. There at the top of the steps was the mousy Druz girl in her uncrumpled mandeel, shaking her fists at the overcast skies and keeping her distance from the barking dogs. We saw there were the stains of tears all over her flowery pinafore and over her open sandals which had been a present from the house. And when one of the salukis came too close she kicked it away and began shouting again at the skies, 'Halas. Halas. Go home. Go home.' But Marlin and Judge were not listening. They had brought up the chopper from the yard and were rushing it at the door of the den, the handlebars twisted round to make a battering-ram. Inside the defiant Trench was cussing hard and lobbing ashtrays and Fanta bottles and bits of pipe far out over the crabgrass lawns below. While Marlin was up close to the door with his crotch over the keyhole Judge was rolling back the chopper for another charge. And all the time the skies were coming down closer. And the dogs were past barking now. They hung their silly heads and fought for breath. And as the smothering migraine skies came down over the spindly minarets of

165

Mzeitbeh and Bab Idriss and over the unstirring umbrella pines of the Harj, down over the black tin roofs of the camps and across the tired greens and fairways of the Golf Club and through the cracked filigree of the Ottoman balconies and into the wheezing air-cons of Pontiacs and Buicks and the suites and bars of the Phoenicia and the Holiday Inn and the shrunken lungs of those lying under the weeping eyes of St Maroun, down over Hamra and the broken corniche, down over Ain Mreisse, I ran away down the cool steps and hid myself right under the crashed Barcalounger in the study, and all the time that great wet-nurse was coming down over the mountains, down over Ain Dara and Bhamdoun and Aley to snuff out the city with her crushing porn dugs.

After we had been beaten we were sent to chapel, to repent. This meant another hour or so of hanging about but I was relieved to part company with my wall. All the gallows humour had subsided now that the beatings were over; we spent our time in desultory gobbing contests and kicking psalters between the pews. The hour was almost up when Palgrave suddenly pranced up to the lectern. He opened with a flurry of air guitar, and followed with his old impression of Alvin Stardust, a 51 stuck into one corner of his mouth doing for a microphone and his arm out-stretched to perform the gesture of the beckoning fist. It was this moment that the headman had chosen to review our consciences, entering from the door to the right of the altar in front of which Palgrave was revolving lubriciously. Though Ferrers and I had scrambled back behind the pews to assume some semblance of expiation, Palgrave continued with his old turn until the headman fell full upon him from behind the lectern.

We followed his blubbing figure back to the study. The second beating was always a different business from the first. Prior tenderness played a part in this, as did the increased vim of the strokes. The privilege of a private audience would now also be withdrawn. We were marched into the study all together. He forced Palgrave down first, holding him by the scrag, and pushing his head into the frowsty armchair. Palgrave was doing his best to pull himself together and not flinch. In situations like this it was not done to watch. The headman brought down his gym shoe from the hook stiff and crusted with old polish and waited while Palgrave hooked up the flap of his jacket. I looked away towards the mantlepiece. There were no invitations there, no urns nor spaniels nor carriage clocks: just a small bowl of fruit which sat there shrinking for a couple of weeks before being replaced. It was curious, this English habit of treating fruit like flowers. Mostly they were just apples and oranges in the headman's bowl, and walnuts in December, though once I was surprised to see a pomegranate there. I had tried to lift the thing needless to say but Fisher had caught me in the corridor and confiscated it on the spot. Before he put it into his pocket he rubbed it with his hanky and told me that it was called a Punic Apple – *Punica granatum*. He said that if I didn't remember what it was called the next time he asked he would report me to the headman; but he never mentioned it again.

After the beating we were shy of each other. We each went to seek out the company of groups we did not usually mix with. For the rest of the day the aura of the double beating would stay with us, and jun-men would come and gape, and others like Barnsley and Standish would want to compare notes and inspect our striae. Like bur in the woods the aura clung to us, and we could not shake it off, though we tried, in different ways. Palgrave sat on the edge of the track despondently chucking in bets and disowning the honour that was due to him. Ferrers sought out Cooke and beat him into the ground, and I went alone down into the lower corridor and ran my fingers along the joints between the photographs and tried to see if I could make

167

out the faces of the double-beaten among them, but of course I could see nothing which marked them out, and suddenly I felt foolish peering into so many dead and unbetraying eyes.

When I returned to the dormitory I found I could not get back in. Savage's new floating-island chariot had become stuck in the door. Assorted slaves were pulling desperately from the front while courtiers and hangers-on pushed from the rear. Above all the commotion Savage reclined in a cradle of pillows and fur, a corona of 9mm. cartridges upon his head, while his favourite nestling beside him swatted intermittently with a palm fan at the backs of the heaving slaves. When one of the slaves lost his balance and slipped under the feet of his fellows both began tittering and pinching each other. The blockage was clearly going down well. But Standish who had designed the floating island in a bid to return to favour was nowhere to be seen. And in the background I caught sight of Cooke, trying to hobble through to the stalled chariot, holding up some ice boxes above the crush. Savage had ordered ice and Cooke was obliging.

all foreign nationals

Omer has still not returned and we have had no news from him for weeks. Down on the front drive the Plymouth sits accumulating snails and sticky carob husks. My father says he doesn't like to drive with the streets as they are.

This afternoon they have been setting up rockets in the field below our house. We have a good view of it all from the lower veranda. While we were eating the kubbeh that Mona had prepared they trundled the launcher in from the corniche. From their fatigues we could tell it was one of the maverick army units that have defected to the Mourabitoun. Immediately they cross the field my father begins frantically telephoning those of his old schoolfriends who have become revolutionaries but most of the lines are still down after last night's shelling from the east. Mona, confused by the tringing of the phone and with the echo of last night's shelling still in her ears, keeps padding through in her bare feet and asking what we are ringing for all the time, and as she leaves the room my father looks at the back of the door and smiles his Voltaire smile and taps his fingers on his forehead. 'Magnouneh,' he whispers, hardening the g as the Egyptians do.

Eventually he puts down the phone and announces that he will go in person to Fakhani and speak with Arafat or the Devil if need be but the Plymouth will not start and so he returns and paces up

171

and down the veranda sipping Amstel and dropping ash over the geraniums. Down in the field the Mourabitoun are holding a press conference. A group of foreign reporters has assembled for the occasion. They are asking questions in English about the weight of the SAM's warhead, and its range and capabilities. In answer to the questions the Mourabitoun men launch one of the missiles north over the water to Jounieh. Halfway across the base of the rocket slips away into the bay and the warhead carries on to the other side, but its impact is lost among the other shells distantly falling over the eastern sector and over the bright-clouded flanks of Sanine. After the demonstration is over a Mourabitoun spokesman wanders over with his hands behind his back and grins at the foreign correspondents. All begin asking their questions at the same time. What is the range of the warhead? Where is its projected deployment? Who has supplied it? When they have piped down the spokesman begins a long and convoluted speech in Arabic about the nobility of the revolutionary struggle and the hard road to freedom. None of the correspondents understand a word of this and call out for a translation. Finally one local journalist steps in. 'The man,' he explains to the foreigners, 'is saying no comment.'

All afternoon I wait on the lower veranda for the launcher to fire again, but nothing happens. At dusk a fat driver with a carbine arrives from Fakhani in a requisitioned service Mercedes. He has come to escort us to rue Hamra where we will be spending the night with friends. Mona clambers in last with the parrot Mikado and immediately starts crossing herself and rubbing her Maroun until my father kicks her and tells her in French to shut up. Beyond the campus the streets are almost empty apart from the heaps of rubbish. Somewhere towards the mountains there is the sound of distant firing, like the pop-pop of maize on a griddle. Outside the stores which have not been burnt out security men loll in looted armchairs with camphor handkerchiefs over their faces. Some are playing trictrac and puffing on narghiles, others are napping. With the masks and the stubble they all look like vexed renderings of Desperate Dan. There are more wheelbarrow men on the streets than cars. They pass *freely between the sectors bringing water-melons, cigarettes, Coca-Cola, canned meats, hashish, gum, whisky, to the snipers and the militiamen. (Each week they bring down to the house cartons of Marlboro, Gordon's Gin, Amstel, tinned asparagus, Grape Nuts and Chiver's marmalade, all looted to order.) Along Hamra some of the old cafés and patisseries are still open though their clientele has changed somewhat. The elegant shoppers and overdressed children have been replaced by chain-smoking fighters with racoon eyes. I look back but they are all Mourabitoun and PFLP in their chocolate anoraks, and no Fatah men from the camps.*

In the morning there is the usual lull in the shelling, and the cafés are full of laughter and high spirits, and the shops are crowded with people gossiping and getting in supplies. We take a taxi back to the campus. The field is empty again, but as we come down into the drive we can see that the house is encircled by groundsmen with brooms. All the windows have been shattered. My mother runs ahead of me through to the dining room but no glass has survived except the decanters in the cracked tantalus half-full of whisky. The house is buzzing with flies, and there are caterpillars and beetles crawling over the fruit bowls and trays of pistachios, and over the remains of broken tumblers and Galet and shards of crystal bowls like explorers among Arctic bergs. She goes from cupboard to cupboard but everywhere it is the same. I find my father standing outside his study holding the door shut as if he were trying to keep out a bad smell. Later I peep through the window and see that all the tall cases in which he displayed his collection of Phoenician glass have been cleared, and only a slab of fulgurite from the Palmyra Desert remains. Over the years he had built up quite a collection, taking duplicates from the university museum. After dinner he liked to remind his guests, many of whom had doubtless heard him speak on the subject before, how the vials and unguent jars and perfume flasks of the Phoenicians had been exported to every corner of the known world, to Gaul, to Southern Iberia and to Cornwall, out through the trading ports of the Black Sea into the wild steppes. Only the

173

Phoenicians knew the secret of creating glass that was not merely translucent but transparent, and by the time of Christ they had established commercial glassworks in Northern Italy and Alexandria, and from there spread their art to Rome and the Saône and the Rhine. Soon the glass workshops of Rome had become so numerous and the smoke from their furnaces such a nuisance that the authorities were obliged to expel them beyond the city walls.

My mother finds him still standing with that winded look outside the study. 'They can do miracles with restoration,' she says, without going into the room. He does not reply, but as she is going he raises his head stealthily, as if above a strafed parapet.

'It's only sand. That's all. Only a fool would worry if they lost sand.'

'Of course, darling. Let's try to have lunch now.' But throughout lunch my father stays in his study, trying to put a call through to my sister in London via the Commodore Hotel where they keep the lines open for the journalists filing copy. And when he comes through for coffee he suddenly seems bent and his age. My mother touches his hand as he sits.

'You can always start again, darling.'

'It's not that. It's Ana. I want to know that something hasn't happened to her.' He takes his coffee back with him to the study, and begins telephoning again.

I returned to find time had grown sluggish in my absence and I had lost the trick of day–dreaming. I saw only what was in front of me and let the machine of bells and routines carry me up through the weeks. I no longer followed the day's trading prices on the blackboard which had been erected at the end of the dormitory. Each week I supplied Standish with a handful of rounds and cartridges and let him deal on commission. He welshed a little of course but I could afford not to notice. As the market had diversified I allowed him to buy into whatever was climbing. Most weeks I did not know whether I was holding Belgian chocolates, or mint Edwardian stamps, or Frisbees and boomerangs. Occasionally we got burnt but that was to be expected.

At the weekends the school seemed almost empty. Those who went down to the woods spent their hours trading up around the lodge while the juniors played among the ruins of the old camp. Few of the juniors had ever seen the boundaries of the woods, and most only half-believed the stories about the camp and the fighters. The horse spirit had all but been forgotten. Even the chariots were losing their hold now that so many juniors had bought their freedom. Sprint races had become more popular than fights, and even there the betting had cooled off as the action had moved over into the Möbius strip and purely speculative investments. Standish and the other traders who held discretionary powers, they were the idols now.

Down at the grass court Ferrers and I kill time playing chicken with a rusty sheath knife. It seems an age since I first hid behind those bushes and watched Duff-Revel deliver his repertoire of winners and marvelled at the variety and sweetness of his shots. Yet the moist grass is still heavy with his spirit and the spirit of his strokes . . . the looping arc of a topspin backhand that faithfully transcribed the drawing of an avengeing sword . . . the herdsman's delicate forward flick . . . volleys with the crisp touch of summary executions . . . the whipping action of his topspin forehand, taming invisible slaves. His game was full of smoke and blood. And even now the grass wore the look of a tended field of the fallen.

The idea was to throw the knife as close to the feet as possible without piercing them. The blade made a rasping noise, scratching pebbles as it went in. After the first few throws Ferrers shut his eyes. He reached down and felt for the knife between his feet, and after he had thrown he waited with his eyes still closed for my reply. Though he didn't say anything I knew he wanted me to close my eyes also. First I just closed them for the throw. The knife landed a little short but the line was right. Then I closed them to receive too. This was more difficult. Ferrers always threw close and hard, sometimes scraping the edge of the wellington. If I flinched just a shade he would pierce right through the rubber. Still I closed my eyes and heard the familiar rasp as the blade went in between my feet. After a few exchanges it became easier, more of a rhythm than a test of nerve. But though I closed my eyes receiving and closed them when I threw I could not keep them closed continually as Ferrers did. I had to have that moment of sight in between.

As long as the blade missed the war would go on. If I flinched or if the blade caught me the war would be over for ever. If the war ended now there could be no victory. I needed the war to go on for Omer's sake and those like him who knew only obscurity and neglect in peacetime, and yet I was sure that if the war continued the airport would be closed again and I would not be able to return home. And the war had begun to chase away much of what I had known as indissolubly part of that home.

The day before I left the fat driver with the M14 had taken me over to the Lindbergh villa to collect my things. All the way I held my nose and when we arrived I felt giddy and out of breath. Only Trench had stayed behind, to finish his medical degree at the AUB, and I found him laid out on the divan which had been piled high with every cushion in the house, staring out at the frangipani in his shorts and flip-flops while the mousy maid who was out of uniform tweezered embers on to the bowl of his tall narghile. He had lost the sweatbands and some of the beads but though his hair was longer, it seemed thinner, darker. When he saw me he gestured with his mouthpiece up the stairs.

Emmy's room looked entirely different with bare walls. All the Snoopy and LOVE posters and pennants of West Coast colleges she had never visited had left only faint outlines, tack holes and solitary books, like aerial photographs of target installations. I picked up my things and padded softly up to the floor of the den. The sign on the door had gone but when I pushed I found the door was locked. Quietly I ran down the stairs again, and out to the waiting car.

The Americans had gone the day after the British left in a convoy of twenty cars fluttering with Union Jacks led by the Embassy Austin Princess and a station wagon containing the bodies of the American Ambassador and his commercial attaché. Their limousine had been found abandoned at the museum crossroads on the way back from the Baabda Palace. It was not long before the bodies had turned up too, without shoes and socks at the beach of Ramlet al-Baida. Emmy and the other Americans were evacuated in a giant landing craft thick with marines which came ashore at the beach club on the corniche. I watched it go from the flat roof out across the bay where we had scanned for sea monsters and giant squids. Before the craft landed the families had lined up quietly along the corniche promenade with their luggage and their pets while the Fatah men looked on, as if they were all waiting on a platform for a train. I had imagined evacuations full of crying and running and darkness, not like this. Most of the foreigners were leaving by cars across the mountains, according to Mona who sees them when she comes back after the weekends crawling in long convoys through Mazra and Chiyah and out beyond the camps. Mona exults in this leaving of foreigners, but this is a city of foreigners and if they all leave the city will be empty. Most of the natives are only foreigners who arrived early. Everywhere there are immigrants, expatriates, itinerants, refugees, double exiles, villagers from the south, from the mountains: most will not leave because they cannot return home. If the rich

177

stay it is because they can afford protection, and if the poor stay it is because they have nowhere else to go.

We managed well enough without glass. We drank out of plastic picnic mugs and the windows were covered in polythene and hardboard. Despite my mother's entreaties my father refused to have the windows replaced. In some ways it was better because the rooms were shadier and cooler too, though Mona cut herself almost every day. Many of the shards were too slight to notice and the darkness did not help matters. I would precede her wearing gardening gloves, sweeping surfaces for the invisible splinters. Once she told me that out in the desert there were whole dunes made of glass. The Bedou kept these places to themselves. The glass was so hard and thick that even a sword would not break it. When the first and last rays of the sun touched the dunes it was as if they had been struck by a giant tuning-fork. The sound carries for miles over the sands and those jackals and gazelles who hear it are struck deaf and the dunes are encircled by their carcasses and the vultures that pick them dry. I told all this to Palgrave when I returned but I am not certain that he believed me.

lawless roads

I had not been looking forward to Sports Day, and when it came I went down to the bottom of the drive ahead of the other boys and sat under the wellingtonia watching for my sister. As the wide coupés and long estates ground their way over the gravel boys would peel off from the waiting group and jump in for the final few yards of the journey. Last year my sister had turned up on a motor bike but this year she had promised to come in a car. Since morning I had been trying to remember what she was calling herself now. Last year it had been Billy, and the year before Saffron.

In the distance I could hear the crack of the starting pistol and the barking of the visiting dogs. After the others had gone I sat on the lowest branch blindly fingering the crossed horse-shoe carvings on the bark of the wellingtonia which had probably been left by Ferrers who often waited in the same tree. And when I had satisfied myself that they were not coming I walked backwards down the drive, light with relief, but a little sore to be seen returning on my own. All along the edge of the fields parents had set up picnic chairs and hampers around their cars. Some had spread jugs of Pimm's and cold meat and salads over the open backs of their estates, others stood about popping open champagne and taking in the action through racing binoculars. Those boys who were ashamed of their parents in some way or other were doing their best to look inconspicuous, tucking in under cover of their cars. I had already resolved to lift any binoculars that came my way.

At the end of the row the Palgraves had established themselves on a tartan rug beside an old Landrover coated rose-red with their Somerset mud. Around them two rose-red cockers chased in hectic circles while Palgrave's mother passed around a thermos and his sisters lay with their backs to each other looking beautiful and embarrassed to be there. Both were wearing brilliant white jeans so tight and pinched that I thought at any moment they might cry out in pain but their unfreckled faces registered only a glowing note of unbelonging. Palgrave himself was nowhere to be seen. His mother was waving, then beckoning. As I approached she fixed me with her piercing beryl stare. 'Tobias. How nice. You remember Perdita, and Petronella.' She gestured towards the girls who shuddered their acknowledgement. She made room on the rug and I squatted down upsetting some plates.

When I was down Palgrave's father shook my hand vigorously and pushed a plate of tartrazine coronation chicken in my direction. 'Get your snout into that, old thing.' He took a quick nip from his flask. 'Harry's off with that Standish fellow. Making a book on the races or something. Of course you're not an athletics man . . . Tennis, isn't it?'

'Well . . .'

'That new Romanian fellow, doesn't know how to lose. Whips up the crowd. At this rate there'll be streakers on centre court next year.'

Over by the science room I could make out a gaggle of juniors arguing beside some figures in white chalk on the wall. From the shadow of a horse-chestnut Cleeve was watching them in his pressed tweed suit, which he wore for special occasions, and a fresh bow-tie, the pages of his notebook flapping in the breeze. I made my excuses and headed off the other way.

The front of the school was thick with pigeons, fat-breasted, scuffling, grey as the air. Not a few of them were circling a purple Beetle parked over the drive under the masters' lodge. I walked across and peered through the dirt-glazed windows. My sister was in there snoozing with the seats down, scrunched together with two other bodies. I tapped on the pane. After much groaning and squirming the bodies separated themselves. They all had short badger-streaked hair and leather jackets which were too small for them and angora sweaters and black drain-pipe jeans. One of the others came round first. Once he had got his bearings he clambered out and shook himself down. He looked at me sideways through shot spirit-level eyes. 'Right, you must be Toby. This is Tina who's at St Martin's with Billy. And I'm Jebb.' Then it was still Billy. His voice was crypto-Cockney, swooning away like bad reception. Tina extended a skinny arm out of the car-fug and when I shook her hand it had the same melting softness as my grandmother's hands.

My sister gets out fiddling with her ear-ring, cocking her head slightly towards her hand as if she is trying to hear something just out of reach. She comes over and kisses me on the nose, and quietly she says, 'Hello, thing. I'm famished; let's all go and have a real lunch.'

By the time we found our way down through the one-way system to the Royal they had stopped serving in the low-lit dining room, but the conservatory was still open for snacks. As we waited for our orders Jebb kept time with some low-grade loutery, kicking out at the Windsor chairs, blowing sugar over the girls, discomforting the local burghers with his language. The girls plucked at their hair with wetted fingers

183

and shared make-up. When he blew some sugar into one of their powders Tina daubed at his cheek with lipstick and he didn't fight back. 'Fuck, Jebb. It's time you went and sorted yourself out,' she said as she painted fat parallel stripes over his cheek. When she had finished Jebb wandered out over the croquet lawn and dropped down on the far bench under the mossy statue where the dogs played during Sunday lunch. He sat very still, hunched up as if he were trying to burrow into the lining of his own jacket. When he returned he had the air of someone who had just been slapped and rather enjoyed it. He was complaisant and droopy and wouldn't touch his food. Ignoring him the girls sucked their way through their cream of asparagus and sundaes which they had ordered to come together, pursing their lips so as not to disturb the drying paint of their masks.

After lunch we left the car and walked over the pedestrian precinct and through the alleys of half-timbered gift shops towards the cathedral. Tina wanted to visit her younger brother who was in his last year at the college. Though the sky is dull and heavy the green in front of the cathedral is filled with shirtless snoggers and tattooed squaddies swilling beer. As we walk down beneath the headstones my sister takes my hand and squeezes it so that I can feel her sharp nails pricking my palm. I am almost her height now so she doesn't need to stoop much when she whispers in my ear, 'Habibi, will you do something for me but you mustn't tell home.' Her breath smelt of the sundae and Turkish cigarettes. I knew already what it would be.

'I haven't saved much this term. Why don't you put a call through again?' I had brought out in an envelope what I intended to give her. That way she wouldn't be able to wheedle more.

'The lines are always down. I got a telex from the Commodore two weeks ago. I'll pay you when they wire

184

my bank.' This was the customary refrain. She hadn't even varied the wording from last time.

'What did they say?'

'Mummy's still stuck in Larnaca. No boats will run to the western sector. Baba won't leave the house. Last time he went to Spinneys they tried to kidnap him.'

'They'd never touch him. It's the new car they're after. And Mona, and Omer?' She was touristically eyeing the flying buttresses above our heads, her throat arched as it used to be when she did back-flips into the pool at the club. Her teeth were clenching impatiently.

'What do you care about that meathead anyhow? It's his sort who are fucking it all up.' Across the close a master in a dog-collar stopped and pretended not to stare. I suppose we must have looked a touch off-beat, three badger-heads with a North Hill boy in a patched sports jacket and itchy grey flannels.

The house where Tina's brother lived on St Michael's Road was built from the same pumice brick as North Hill but inside the largest rooms had been divided into warrens of narrow passages and study cubicles with wooden partitions and draperies hung between. The effect was somewhere between a souk and a shanty town though the predominant smell was not spices but bad milk and sweaty games clothes. Tina seemed to know her way through the maze. As we followed her, like apples in a tub pale faces bobbed up from behind curtains and quickly disappeared again. Inside the boys seemed too large for their tiny cubicles. It made me think of pets waiting to be chosen.

We threaded our way into the senior annexe where the studies were ampler, about the size of monks' cells, and fitted with proper doors. As we passed I peered through into the dark incense-filled chambers where older boys lounged on threadbare sofas and hammocks playing cards and smoking roll-ups. Tributary music tumbled out of each open door into the roiling sound-river of the corridor. None of the etiolated figures within paid the slightest attention as we tramped through their nether world. We found Tina's brother at the end of the corridor throwing darts into a poster of Stonehenge. He cleared some surfaces and we perched while he fussed with tea and mugs with broken handles. His hair was *en brosse* and possibly dyed but as yet unbadgered. There was one sticky Club left hidden behind some history books which he presented to me. While I sucked it the others chatted on about lead singers and clothes and venues. I nodded along and smiled whenever the others laughed.

After a while Jebb stops joining in and slouches on the windowsill picking the inside-out stickers off the window pane. Though it is the middle of the afternoon the curtains are tightly closed. Suddenly everyone has stopped talking. Tina's brother is looking at Jebb with mild disbelief, as if he had just picked open a large scab.

'But they're my Roadhogs.' He says this in a surprisingly high pitch. Jebb rises from the sill painfully and steps back towards the door, but gradually, ponderously, as if he were walking under water. He backs out, his arms pulling at the carved lintel.

'Don't grief me, right. Who's going to clock them anyway with the curtains closed.'

'Some days I open them.'

'Right. Sure. Don't choke. I'm out of here. My cock's got a gig in town tonight.' The girls watched the receding short jacket and the shiny arse and put their fingers down their throats. Tina's brother just gaped at the black window.

'Don't worry about him.' His sister stroked the feathery tips of his hair. He acts like a roadie but really he's a poet.' Her brother flicked his head away.

'That's hardly an excuse.' He ran his fingers over the

186

books on his shelves which all had their spines facing the wall. This seemed to console him.

For a while longer we sat finishing our tea while Jebb paced up and down outside in the corridor. Over in the corner by the window there is the poster of the skull with the flowers growing out of it, the same as the one in the den. Both rooms belong to the same underworld tucked close under the surface, a place without issue or deliverance. If I peeled away the poster I would surely find a secret passage which would lead eventually into the den itself. But when I look more closely I notice that the paper is riddled with countless tiny holes, as if the termites had been at it. More filter than picture.

Jebb led our Indian file back through the narrow turns of the study bazaar. We passed among peeping troglodyte faces and deep inscriptions in long-extinct filigreed scripts. Somewhere Jebb must have taken a wrong turning because before long we came out above a buried yard, sealed with wire-netting so that balls would not wander. Some boys were playing a casual game of wall cricket, the stumps chalked on to the cratered brickwork behind the batsman. All had the cautious and watched air of juniors though some were almost as tall as men. To one side of the yard I recognized the annexe from which we had just set out. Above the row of darkened studies in a bow window which served as a gallery a group of older boys reclined in collapsed armchairs drinking from paper bags and surveying the proceedings below.

As I look up towards this gallery the sun emerges for the first time and the figures above are framed in blinding aureoles. Something about the arrangement and detail of their hollow outlines signals that I should not scrutinize further. I turn away. The others have already gone back into the buildings, and as I follow I look up into the light one last time and see the impossible vision of Duff-Revel with a silly fringe parked lightly on the lap of one of the seniors. Whoever he is never looks down through the netting as the others do. His head and shoulders stretch into the sky at a sniffing incline, like the stone mastiff on a gate. Such a haughty neck. It is impossible to imagine it at any other angle. The burnished husk of him was all that was left, and that even drawn tight and dilated from the grotesque possession within it. And now for the first time I knew that the means existed to extinguish the life of certain wild beasts without scathing their precious hides.

When I returned Ferrers was waiting in the trunk room. There was a book open on his knees but there was too little light to read by and he had not brought out the rubber torch he kept hidden under the floorboards with his radio, his cuttings and sheath knives. Once he had smelt that I was holding something back from him he began to prise into the course of my day with a light but sure touch, as if he were handling one of those fragile puzzles made in the People's Republic of China which Standish had been knocking out the previous summer; after all there might have been bad news from home. I told him everything, much as I have put it down here, omitting only the visit to the yard. When I finished he asked only if I believed Omer had gone south to fight the Israelis. As so often with such questions it was my garrulous failure to answer that he encouraged. Though the idea of Omer returning to our former picnic grounds made perfect wanton sense of my memories. But I could not picture him at the postcard destinations though there were Fatah men in all these places, camped among the poplar trees and alongside the Roman bridge beneath the snows of Mount Hermon, sheltering from the bitter winds on the ramparts of Beaufort Castle, shooting off their Katyushas among the poppy fields and wadis of the Arkoub where the hibiscus roses were as bright as flares in the night. No, if he was there at all, he would have chosen that bald unsheltered hilltop where we used to stop for water-melons on our way out to Marjayoun. The village would be deserted now. With its white church, one bar, low adobe houses and dusty corrals, it had that Mexican feel about it: a ghost pueblo with an unbroken view all the way across the Litani and deep into the forbidden valley of Galilee, the Golan hovering like stacked cumulus on the horizon. The youths in his care would have long dirty hair, T-shirts and flared jeans, and he would probably despise them though they would never know this. In the heat of the afternoon he would lead them out through the untended orange groves with their spare scimitar magazines taped on to the sides of their assault rifles. There would be no Israelis to shoot at, a few of their Maronite stooges perhaps. Still I felt envious of these boys only a few years older than myself. They might never learn the knack of firing an AK47 straight but they had a better chance than most with such an *oustaz*.

'Is there an infallible mark, do you think?' Ferrers asked before we left the trunk room. 'You know – on a man who has killed. Or a move that always betrays him, like a tell in poker.' This was Ferrers' version of continuity, filler talk for the gaps between what really interested him. 'They say' (we were worming our way out through the narrow spaces between the piled trunks) 'that it's different when you can actually see what you've fired into. You develop fish eyes, unlit, filmy.'

'That's the look all the old boys in the photographs have and none of them have killed.' Ferrers pretended not to hear this. He was letting the secret cup of his reading spill a little as we crawled forward through the dark.

'In Corsica or the Pampas where a man has already

189

ransomed his life to his honour, every man in the village has the fish eye, old and young.'

'Then what marks out the killers from those who have yet to kill?'

'Like the martyrs, the suicide bombers who have been shaved and cleansed, they're apart. Pure.'

'Except that Mona says that most of them just do it for the girls, and the Houris later. Ergo the fishy look. It's all those nights of porking and doping.'

'You haven't twigged. As per usual, Shady. I only said that men of honour were *like* martyrs. As the martyr is betrothed to death, so the man of honour is willing to sacrifice himself to his own honour. Both stand apart from all the others who just cling and crawl like wretched dung beetles.'

stopped counting broken truces

That last year for the first time the corridors and dormitories and gardens were filled with music. No place was free of it. The nights were restive with the mosquito-buzz of furtive trannies. More powerful machines would ambush the stillness of rooms with sudden top-volume sallies, like the abrupt barkings of a hidden dog, and then as quickly die away. Even in the attics under the doors of the younger matrons the acoustic glop seeped out and into the hearts of those who loitered there. Around every corner there were slushy refrains and sweet desperations. Nowhere was safe from the love hooks, this candy of yearning and pleading and moaning which rotted even the sharpest teeth.

In the first weeks Ferrers, supported by a band of senior Hounds and Curlews, had waged a vigorous campaign against the transistor radios, mounting sound patrols across the dormitories and gardens, probing the bog-houses and music cubicles for headphone solitaires. But this purge had proved a victim of its own success. Such quantities of equipment were confiscated in those first weeks that the trading values of all batteries and every species of tranny soared to levels which ensured that extortion and racketeering among the sound patrollers rapidly became endemic. It was even mooted that Standish had provoked Ferrers into orchestrating the war against the trannies with only this end in mind. Whatever the truth of this, by the end of the first month of the campaign the black trade in Sonys and Philips and Panasonics and Ever-Readies of all specifications had reached such a feverish pitch that one set might be confiscated from a junior in the morning and change hands half-a-dozen times on the floor of the washroom before being ransomed back that night to the same junior for over six times its original trading price. In short, while the sound patrols were kept up there was a tranny bonanza the like of which may never be seen again.

And the sound patrollers were compromised in other ways too. For their ears became precisely sensitized to those love-sickly melodies which it had been their mission to silence. Soon they had begun to whistle and hum. It reminded me of the way my grandmother would siffle out the previous night's jingles, as if she were expelling bad air. By the third week the sound patrollers were being ventriloquized, parasited by the hook-worms. As they went about their business the itch of the worms became too much to bear. They sought sudden delirious release. Out would ooze an *oo-oo-ooh now baby please don't go* or a *come up and see me make me smi-ile/ do what you want running wi-ild*. If observed some patrollers would contrive to convert these slippages into gross parodies, while others trusted that their outbursts could not be interpreted in any other manner. Predictably such parodies were imitated by impressionable jun-men and evolved in time into a specialized genre of disco-cabaret patronized by some of the senior Stags and Buffaloes.

As the tranny crisis worsened Ferrers abandoned himself to random and brutal attacks on his own fallen sound patrollers. Whenever he chanced upon one of the patrollers alone at night in the corridors and on the stone stairways he would wrest the tranny from under their jacket or dressing-gown and club them with it before hurling the thing from the nearest window. Sometimes the machines landed softly in the rain-soaked beds and played on down in the darkness.

One night Ferrers broke into the carpentry shed and fetched out the largest mallet there. That same night he fell upon every tranny he could find in the dormitories and in the washrooms. For days afterwards the floors were littered with fragments of circuit-boards, striped transistor tubes like ancient rock-hard chewing gum, crushed elements and speakers. By the time an effective response had been mobilized he had blockaded himself in the trunk room where he remained for the rest of the night. Again there were those who believed that Ferrers' rampage had already been sanctioned by Standish, and it cannot be denied that in the weeks following the attack Standish retained an almost total monopoly on the supply of trannies. Certainly it was only the circulation of such rumours during the course of the night that saved Ferrers from the full force of the mob outside the refectory the following morning.

Though Ferrers' legendary invulnerability in combat was never tested, he would never lead again. His isolation as *Ferret Furioso* the school bogeyman was now ensured. The moment had come for Standish and Palgrave to make their move, and by the morning break they had called immediate and unprecedented popular elections, promising to end forthwith all repressive and extortionate sound patrols, and protect the trading rights of all juniors against arbitrary attacks from freebooters and maverick strongmen such as Ferrers. The combination of Standish's tactical experience and Palgrave's universal flummery proved irresistible. For the remainder of that last year Standish and Palgrave would rule together in an uneasy coalition. Cooke, who by right of seniority in age had automatically acceded to the position of patrol leader, was quietly sidelined. His status as patrol leader of the Hounds would become purely symbolic, recognized only by masters, and in official school protocol such as the roster during parades and the seating order in the refectory and in chapel. Having conceded his traditional fiscal prerogatives to the new alliance Cooke could no longer afford to retain a court or the services of quippers and favourites; he survived on a small allowance from Standish which he squandered on hiring out the new rickshaw chariots which were drawn about by single jun-men. The old racing chariots had all but disappeared now. Former champions were reduced to taximen, plying for hire along the same corridors where they had once raced.

That Christmas I could not return home. There had been more fighting around the airport. On the day we broke up there was a card from Emmy, with a photograph, probably sent at the prompting of her mother. For the next five years I would receive similar cards, each accompanied by a single photograph. In this first one she appeared in a chequered lumberjack shirt and spray-on jeans tucked into cowboy boots, outside a snowbound house in Maine. I remember wondering if she was aware at the time that this shot was going to be sent out at Christmas, or whether it was selected later, and if the same snap was included in all the cards she had sent out. She had taken the trouble to make every one of the unjoined letters a different colour. She must have almost come to the end of her set of Caran D'Ache.

Her hair had lost its whiteness, and her face was paler, fuller, as were her hips, once narrower than mine, now swelling out of the impossibly tight jeans. Although, as in the studio portraits of the past, the clothes and setting would change over the years, the pose itself (full-length, left thumb in hip pocket, her face upturned a fraction towards the lens) would remain precisely the same. The next snap would show her standing in her bedroom among the staffage of old toys and dolls. The following year she would appear at a roller-disco with spangles on her jeans and on her cheeks. Another year she was at some kind of a pageant, a rhinestone tiara in her now faun hair, some razzmatazz with floats and trumpets going on behind. The final picture would be taken back in front of the house again, the blackness of her leathers lustrous with the brilliance of the snow. In this last her hair was layered and dyed a lizard green in tufts. Despite the incipient toughness I noticed that she had not lost her crescent-moon hairclip. It was pinned like a brooch to her rocker lapel and catching the winter sun . . . Flicking through the six snaps and there it is, some fairground magic, the staccato of a cartoon pupation, her body inflating as if from some ultimately fatal pressure within.

Ferrers had warned me that his parents didn't much celebrate Christmas but when we entered the house high on Frognal Hill there was holly all the way up the banisters and glistening balls hanging on every plant and an enormous Christmas tree covered in silver lanterns each with a small red candle inside. Despite pretending to insouciance during the tube journey up from Waterloo I had been unable to conceal my unfamiliarity with the ticket machines and skittish disorientation among the crowds through which Ferrers had weaved with expert precision, skimming past attaché cases and shopping bags when the going got tight. Fortunately while forging ahead he had not witnessed my pussy-footing around the teeth of the escalator, nor my gaping awe at the bright profusion of the tunnels. Neither of his parents was home when we arrived but Ferrers had his

own key. It was a towering, cluttered place, the house, with
stained-glass windows on the landings and worn-through
carpets on the stairs. As we ascended each floor was
noticeably shabbier and less decorated than the last. At
the top the staircase narrowed considerably and there was
black-and-white-checked lino on the floors and bare light
bulbs and shrivelled mushroom wallpaper. Ferrers pushed
open one of the doors with his foot. The room inside was
piled high with cardboard boxes for electrical goods and
empty bird cages and rolls of polythene sheeting. 'This used
to be where the caretaker lived. Now the whole place is
filling up with junk room by room. They won't let anything
go,' Ferrers explained a little sheepishly.

His own room was magnificent and empty except for
neatly ordered shelves filled with books about the Nazis and
the Middle East, a giant sagging *chaise-longue* under a
branched spotlight, and a child's white wooden bed. The
sloping walls were covered only in maps, some historical,
some road maps, some Ordnance Survey and tourist city-
plans. The back windows looked down on to the sunless
garden where long strips of guttering and rusting gas
cylinders lay in the deep grass. On what had once been
the terrace an ancient dormobile rested up on blocks. It
appeared to be crammed full of more polythene sheeting.
Through the front windows lay the now lighted plains of the
city, extending formidably to every visible horizon, as
limitless and indifferent as the sky above the desert. It
was a chilling spectacle, vertiginous, but glorious also.
'My mother says I'm lucky because having a view is the
privilege of the poor in London.' As Ferrers spoke I
remembered the comforting squalor of Nido tins and
broken fruit boxes under the fly-blown date palms along
the airport road, and I remembered too the forgotten guard
and wondered what could have become of him.

Ferrers' parents seemed too young to have accumulated so

much old rubbish, and much younger than I remembered them from their Sunday-morning vigils outside chapel. Both parents greeted me almost too politely, as if they had been expecting someone else. Of the two, Ferrers' mother appeared to be slightly the older, probably in her mid-forties, and this impression of seniority was reinforced by the simultaneously puckish yet well-lunched presence of the father. The mother wore her hair severely brushed back off her forehead and no make-up, and tailored slacks which complemented her attenuated figure. The almond eyes, long dark eyelashes, the grooved sharpness of the features: there was much of her in Ferrers, and little obviously from the father whose easy and passive alertness was that of a man on holiday in his own house. There was an insistent tenderness between Ferrers and his mother too which was wholly unanticipated. Much to his embarrassment she fusses over the state of his flannels and his jacket while the father seems to shrink like a tortoise into his large city collar and cuffs. As she takes a tissue from up her sleeve and wipes some stains from his neck she puts her nose into his thick hair and sniffs. Then she wrinkles up her nose exaggeratedly as if she had just smelt something awful and pecks him gently where the whorl of thick hair sprouts from his nape.

We are allowed to have dinner with the parents, and to my astonishment we are offered wine with our goulash, and black coffee after our cheese and biscuits. At first I cannot follow the conversation at all. Who can this ubiquitous Sarah and Bernard possibly be? I conclude they must be cousins or close family friends. It is only after some sweaty calculations that I finally grasp that the family refer to each other by their first names. After dinner we are left to load the dishwasher, and Sarah and Bernard disappear off upstairs. I keep putting the plates and glasses in the wrong slots which creates extra work for Ferrers but surprisingly he doesn't grouse about it. For a moment while we are clattering around with the plates

I imagine I hear lazy guitar chords drifting down from somewhere above us, but then the sound is lost as the machine starts chugging.

We were left to our own devices during the day. Sarah taught at the Institute of Developmental Psychology and Bernard sat on advisory committees in the City. Neither of them would return before seven in the evening. Sometimes we would play chess or Risk in the attic room, but most days we went up to the Heath. Ferrers knew the ways to avoid other walkers. Sometimes we would go for hours and see nobody. Sometimes we would follow certain walkers for miles without quite letting them see us. We would try to spook them by cracking branches just behind them and making calls across their path and inscribing ominous words in the mud along their route. Ferrers knew all the best spying trees from which we could prospect for victims. He could tell from some distance, even by the gait alone, what particular species of walker we had in our sights and the likely route they would be taking. Ferrers had his own typology of solitary walkers. There were *naturalists*, *regulars*, *poets*, *prowlers* and *queers*. Sometimes the categories crossed. Everywhere we went across the Heath, on the rocks and benches and on the barks of trees, I would see the same familiar cursive signs and inscriptions. Some of the markings on the barks, like long-healed scars, had puckered and stretched with the years.

Occasionally we would emerge from the Heath at a crossroads beside a long tall white wooden building which faintly resembled a Mississippi paddle-steamer. Here we would cross over and head down into a small wood bordered on one side by houses and on the other by a road which could still be heard from within through the crisp winter air. Few walkers used the wood, and Ferrers' markings were at their most visible and insistent here. On

200

our first visit, after we had passed a little way beyond a black half-frozen pond, Ferrers had casually pointed up to a tree and told me that it was there that he had once situated his base. Around the tree there was the black sludge of dead leaves and a canopy of high skeletal beeches blocking out the light. It was a place very like the crater in Hobson Wood. The base itself was still well camouflaged from below, but long abandoned. When we climbed up there was recently dated crush graffiti everywhere and butts and beer cans all over the boards. Before we went Ferrers kicked away a couple of the supporting struts, but left the platform balancing in the crux of branches.

Two days before we were due to return Ferrers went off to a check-up at the dentist. It was a biting day. The heating did not come on until much later. I had no experience with coal fires and thought it better not to experiment. I wandered from room to room, unable to find anywhere warm to settle. Like Ferrers' parents, everything in the house was younger than it seemed. There were no antiques or inherited pieces, but most of the furniture was more scuffed and worn than any antique would ever be. They had amassed a great deal, much of which was neither picturesque nor useful. Almost every room in the upper storeys was crammed full with objects and materials which would almost certainly be thrown out or passed on from more conventional house-holds. Yet none of this was betrayed by the lower inhabited floors which were comfortable and modern, though perhaps too functional to be quite fashionable. Both Sarah and Bernard had their own large studies. In Bernard's room the clutter-bug had already begun to assert itself, filling shoe-boxes with sweet tins and jam jars and yoghurt cartons and diverse other small potential containers, and heaping yellow-ing mounds of the *New Statesman* and the *Listener* against the empty walls. A large stereo gramophone cabinet with two tall sentry-box speakers stood in front of the window, debarring the winter light. It was the type of room that did not encourage much further investigation.

Sarah's study was wider, starker, dominated by high beetling bookshelves filled with the dullest sort of textbooks with titles like behaviourist pub signs. *The Blind Response. Fear and Mice. The Reasonable Monkey*. Even here the clutter-bug had been at work, piling up dead stationery – dry Quink pots, petrified Tipp-Ex, broken staples, withered typing ribbons, superannuated Bics and markers – all over the shelves: offerings at the shrine of a finicky ink god. A connecting door went through to the bedroom. I hesitated a little before entering, though when I had gone through I found nothing that they might have preferred to have kept hidden. The colours were stronger, more vibrant than elsewhere in the house, black bamboo framing the mirror, a lime-green candlewick spread, tangerine swirls on the bed-head, but otherwise the furnishings were of the same functionalist type as downstairs. There was less obvious evidence of hoarding here, though the open bathroom door revealed shampoo bottles and squidged-up tubes massing around the basin, and the dressing table was covered in empty Kleenex boxes and pots of skin cream. But otherwise the room was uncluttered. Beside the dressing table over by the window on an inlaid table of the same height there was a single small patch of antiquity. Two nineteenth-century silver handmirrors were arranged around a series of engraved silver powder jars and hairbrushes beneath an oval rocaille frame with a photograph of a wiry woman in a well-cut coat with fox furs around her neck; in her gloved hand she was holding a lead which disappeared, tightly, outside the picture. At the bottom of the photograph was the faint pencil inscription: *Mütti, Prinzregentenplatz*, '32. It was understandable that Ferrers had never mentioned his

German relatives. All the Heil Hitlers and finger-moustaches, the whole hexachord of Jerry brocking, it would have been intolerable.

We returned to find the trannies multiplied and bolder. And today when I hear one of the sugared melodies of those years all I see is the melancholy figure of Cooke, his puissance gone, swishing backwards and forwards alone in his rickshaw chariot down that long unquiet corridor.

continued attacks by unknown assailants

There was a growing sense of detachment in those last terms. This was not a light, giddy feeling, but airless, close, as if all that had once been familiar was now being wrapped in Bernard's rolls of transparent polythene. Slowly, as the layers were added, the sounds within became muffled, the shapes more difficult to make out. But it was we the leavers who had become enveloped in our own ever shrinking circles of concentration. We marked time. We watched flies crawl and cracks widen. We stared at words without reading them. We revised for our exams with the anxious dedication of poor emigrants saving for their passage out. Only thrifty and methodical memory work would secure our indeterminate future. We knew the names of the schools we had been put down for, but little else about them. It was a dead reckoning when we pictured what lay ahead.

In the dormitories there was nothing to divert us from our own stupefaction. Since the treaties had been signed with the Stags and the Curlews raids had become so infrequent that it was no longer necessary to post look-outs or practise defence drills. With the threat of raids, ambushes and arbitrary confiscations receding, swappers and traders had even begun to travel without guards between the wash-

rooms and the dormitories. The sudden scarcities and wild
bonanzas of the past had given way to a regular supply and
demand for trannies, batteries, cassettes, Swiss and Belgian
chocolates, and collectables such as stamps, coins and football
cards; one of the discreet emblems of Palgrave's new power
was the framed collection of Saints cards that hung above his
bed: in return for a small consideration Palgrave permitted
juniors to tack up posters of polar bears, Charlie's Angels and
James Hunt's Maclaren, anything in fact except other
football teams. The Möbius strip and floodlit Subuteo still
attracted some betting, but most of the jun-men preferred
just to watch from the comfort of their beds where they
spent the evenings alone reading Malcolm Bradbury and
Arthur C. Clarke with a tranny buzzing on the chest top.
Now persistent scrappers would be banished to Coventry by
popular vote. Such orders could only be revoked by
common consent at the bi-weekly assemblies when everyone except the new men squatted on top of their chests to
denounce swap cheats and tranny saboteurs and press for
lower taxation on collectables such as stamps and coins.
Sometimes we allowed Cooke and Girl to take shelter with
us in the trunk room during these fractious gatherings.
There we would revise by torchlight and plot late into
the night.

My appointment as chapel prefect brought little power
and few privileges. My duties were limited to slotting up the
hymn and psalm numbers and taking care of the vestry. I sat
alone out in a one-man pew on that over-polished threshold
between the raised altar and the remainder of the congrega-
tion. I was the drum major of devotion. When I knelt the
school fell shuffling to its knees. When I closed my hymnal a
hundred and fifty hymnals closed thunderously behind me.
If I rose out of cue the multitude would rise up also as if to
applaud the show. On the few occasions that Standish and
Palgrave bothered to attend chapel, they would occupy my

vestry somewhat in the manner of a private box. The door of
the vestry, situated to the left of the altar, opened inwards
and any activities there were visible only to the congrega-
tion; the headman sat on the podium beside the lectern, and
the organist played with his back to the service. Those
within would sometimes take advantage of this blindness to
stage quick-change numbers. When the headman came to
that section of the school prayer where the North Hiller
defends his three stumps of Purity, Bravery and Truth against
the Devil who is bowling, the door would slowly swing
open to reveal Standish and Palgrave robed in the Sunday
vestments, brandishing monstrances and swilling on communion decanters. And then as an earnest jun-man read out
the *Here am I; send me* lesson from Isaiah they would be back
again under a pair of surplices shaking like funtime spooks.
Whenever their appearances touched off giggle ripples the
headman would peer down at my island pew; no doubt he
expected to catch his coryphaeus playing the fool.

That last term we slept in Hobson Lodge. Previously we had
not been thought responsible enough as a patrol to enjoy this
privilege which had been shared between the Stags and the
Buffaloes. We occupied the ground floor only where iron
beds and emulsioned chests had been lined up against the
high walls and french windows. The upper floors were
deserted except for the young matron who occupied a small
flat at the top. All the other doors on the upper floors had
been padlocked and painted over. Each evening we would
assemble outside the school and the duty master would
escort us across the Sarum Road and down the drive
overgrown with summer weeds before dismissing us on
the small green beside the lodge. Increasingly Ferrers would
allow Cooke and Girl to join us in the cellars which we were

able to secure from within with a stave. It was here that boys had once searched for an opening to that tunnel the entrance of which was still believed to lie under the war memorial in the upper gardens. But Ferrers was not interested in talk of this kind. And when he was not revising he liked to taunt Cooke with mirages of lost vassalage and fealty and called him *poltroon* and *dung beetle*. Yet Cooke appeared almost relieved to be addressed in this free manner, perhaps because for the first time he had been liberated from the tyranny of his own name.

The cellars were close and sweaty, but if there were rats we never saw any. At one end there was the great black oil-fired boiler which provided the hot water for the matron's room and the one washroom downstairs. Ferrers had bagged the narrow ledge beneath it which he lit with candles lifted from the headman's dining room and three *clobber sticks* bound together with gaffer tape to make a spotlight under which he would bone up on his history; every evening he would slip ahead of the march down from the Sarum Road to raid the trannies in the dormitory for fresh supplies of Ever-Readies. When he was taking a breather from his noting he would direct his three-barreller straight at Cooke who sat huddled up at the other end trying to do his own revision. The ensuing exchanges were always more or less the same. To begin with Cooke would pretend to ignore the dazzling, but eventually when Ferrers did not relent Cooke would tentatively thank him for providing the extra light. This was what Ferrers had been waiting for.

'Don't answer back, fleabag.' He would bring the three-barreller in a little closer.

'But you didn't say anything.'

'Ha. Insolence. From a dung beetle.' And closer still would come the torches.

'No. I promise. It wasn't.'

'Well, well. The cockchafer speaks again.'

210

Cooke kept it shut this time, but not for long because Ferrers would kick his hands away if he tried to shield himself from the three-barreller hovering around his face. Then it was only a matter of a moment or two before Cooke cracked and balled out, 'I submit. I submit.' The beams of the torches would spin away over blistered walls, perspiring pipes, foxed laundry bills.

'YOU submit. YOU.' Ferrers raised his voice, and this was rare. 'YOU. Suzerain Lord of the Hounds, SUBMIT. That's a fine one.' Ferrers spun the torches faster and faster. 'Submit, YOU. Flob on your birthright you mean. Turd over your puissance. What a base thing you are. Less than a zit on the great Duffer's memory.' All the room was visible now in the whirling strobe of the torches, mildewed tunnel vaults above, the stave wedged up against the door, the dark bulk of the boiler. 'SUBMIT. That's what scullies do. That's a schnorrer word.'

'What's that? A schnorrer,' piped up Girl.

'That,' and for just an instant Ferrers stopped whirling and let the beams linger again on Cooke's blithely smirking face, 'that is a man who forgets who he is and fetches up being brocked in a cellar.'

In the third week of term, when shirt-sleeve order was declared and the old bog-houses had released their marshy vapours through the lower corridors, we began to find the tracks of horse-shoes in the grass outside the lodge and in the dry mud along the drive. Not knowing the old stories, the juniors were more curious than afraid. They tried to follow the tracks into the woods. They searched the abandoned stables at the back of the lodge for droppings and straw but found nothing except some old tyres and a cache of sodden staves. As the tracks always appeared in the morning Palgrave organized a series of watches through the night. Predictably there were false-alarms and hoaxes. One night Germ was found outside the french windows with a pair of coconut halves from the Green Room. The following evening the watch followed a faint whinnying noise into the edge of the woods only to discover Girl skulking in the bushes. By popular edict both were banished indefinitely to Coventry. The juniors were taking their search for the horse seriously. A tape-recorder was left out near the freshest trail of tracks. The next morning there were more tracks nearby, but the Philips had been crushed.

The week before our exams were due to start, when interest in the horse was still running high, Palgrave and Standish summoned a special meeting of the dormitory and announced that all upper storeys of the lodge had been placed out of bounds until further notice. Everyone assumed they must be revising in one of the locked rooms and did not wish to be disturbed. In their absence some stayed indoors reading alone and listening to the love glop while others joined the horse patrols that followed the wider paths through the lower woods in search of clues. Already they had begun to find faint tracks and what appeared to be dried-out droppings down on the western side of the woods, away from the drive and the lawns around the lodge. Rumours of a substantial prize from an anonymous benefactor for the first corroborated sighting of the horse were also now fuelling the search. On those long summer evenings I stayed up at the lodge listening for the news from the trannies. Sometimes there were reports from the south. The same blank refrains. They barely bothered to alter the wording from week to week. *Palestinian guerrillas have ambushed a unit of Maronite militiamen south of Tyre . . . An Israeli border-post has been attacked by a suicide bomber . . . last night it was reported that Katyusha rockets were fired into Northern Galilee.* As long as there was no news from the city I would be able to go home

212

after the exams were over. Ferrers had made me promise that this time I would take him with me. Every night in the cellars he made me swear that I would show him all the secret arsenals and shooting-ranges hidden under the camps. And though most of what I had told him over the years about the chambers under the camps was pure invention, every night in the cellars I swore that I would take him there and show him everything.

I remember the day before the exams began was hot and dry. Musson had sent me back to the lodge to pick up some books I had forgotten. There was no breeze in the lank grass along the banks of the drive. When I walked through the empty lodge I could hear nothing but the cooing of pigeons out on the lawns and the burble of a tranny from somewhere high up in the house. The day possessed a languorous stillness which I would not have noticed were I not already hurrying away from it. As I reached the shady hallway I stopped and stood at the foot of the great staircase, stroking the banister. The stained oak was cool to the touch. I padded softly upwards. The corridors on each floor were narrow and dark, but light enough for me to make out each doorway clearly. All the doors on the first floor were still painted over. On the second floor it was the same. None of the rooms had been entered. The matron's door was at the end of the passage. I edged forwards through the sickly music, trying not to breathe in the dry, sporous air. When I was outside the door I knelt down. It was one of those tall old-fashioned pawn-shaped keyholes, like looking through an Islamic arch. At first I did not recognize the matron out of her smock. I thought it must be someone else entirely, and for some moments I fumbled to explain the presence of this intruder to myself while my knees ached to keep their hold on the rough floorboards. She had opened her window and was lying on her back facing the sun. The rippleless flesh between her bright cotton halter-top and frayed jean-shorts was the colour of milk in shadow – when one can no longer tell whether the surface of the jug is liquid or skin. She was still, but restlessly still, like the model of Gulliver at the back of Billings & Edmonds. It was as if she had been tucked too tightly into an invisible bed, as if the silky net of the music had spun her into itself, the love crampons holding her fast. I waited, and when she did not move I crept away. I did not know then that this was the last time I would look upon such a body without understanding what I must desire from it.

When the exams were over there was only waiting left. We paced on our ledge in the clouds, not caring to look back at the distance we had covered, unsighted by routines and reveries from the prospect ahead, too impatient to conjure it into being. The queues at this border post were long and slow, enough to make dullards of the boldest. Some took the waiting out on the country they were leaving. Beakers of formaldehyde in the science room were smashed with retort stands, their pale contents left to the terrapins. Tyres were slashed. Bog-houses were blocked and flooded. The lantern-bearers found work for themselves. Every morning I would discover psalters ripped in the vestry, surplices damp with spittle, the host disturbed. I did not mention my finds for fear of more parades.

A week after the exams had ended fresh tracks were discovered leading down from the lawns into the western side of the woods. The tracks had not been there that morning when Magyar took parade outside the lodge. After we had been dismissed, and Magyar had gone back up the drive, the entire patrol headed down into the woods,

214

jun-men scrapping and jostling to keep ahead of the pack. It had rained hard the night before and the tracks were clearly marked, though once we came down into the long grass in the central clearing they became more difficult to follow. Palgrave ordered that the patrol fan out into a line and move forward at the same pace. The long grass had been trampled in several transecting lines so it was by no means obvious which way the animal had taken, though all the lines were beginning to converge westwards, towards the ruined house. As we neared the boundary the grass thinned. The tracks ran straight out, clear as print, across the chicken-wire fence and over the wasteground to the fallen elm. After the elm there was more rank grass and nettles, and the shell of the house beyond.

Palgrave held up his arm and pulled the patrol to a halt; some had already crossed into the wasteground and were clambering over the rotting branches. Then everyone turned and saw Girl waving his arms wildly at the end of the line. He had picked up the tracks again heading back into the upper part of the clearing. Palgrave almost lost his balance as the line broke up and charged past him to where Girl stood waving. A scrum of jun-men was following the tracks back through the woods and on to what was little more than a goat path which criss-crossed up the face of the bank. At the same time Palgrave was trying to force his way through to the front of the column but the path was narrow and the juniors would not make way. Some had slipped shrieking down into the high nettles and others were braving the sheer bank, clawing their way up through the wet earth. Then we came out at the top of the bank and the tracks were clearly visible again, leading straight across the lawns into the lodge.

Inside the juniors were silent. The tracks led through the dark hallway into the dormitory. Nobody had turned the lights on but I could make out the muddy prints of horse-shoes over the beds and the walls and the french windows and the ceilings. Beds had been upturned and taken apart. Shampoo and toothpaste were smeared over sheets and mattresses and tartan rugs and clothes from the chests which lay capsized over the floor, their drawers heaped against the wall. The trading blackboard, festooned with streamers of cassette tape, had been brought down on several trannies whose innards rolled about under the feet of the juniors who trailed up and down the room, not speaking or touching anything, like visitors at an exhibit. It required special attention to take it all in. The chaos cried out for the reverence accorded to a new creation. And there was not a little wonder on their junior faces as they studied all the particulars, the one-off effects, all the exquisite diffractions. There was the manner, for example, in which the horse-shoes appeared at some stage to have become coated in chocolate and then had pranced merrily on over floored polar bears and Saints cards and pages of Sci-Fi and mint coronations of George V. And the curious way in which the Möbius strip had been chewed into a gnarled double helix still dripping with globules of pearly saliva. And again, the shredding of the Subuteo field and the systematic dismemberment of the players from their hemispherical bases with only the stretcher-bearers standing and intact. This lantern-bearer was a humorist evidently.

In the days that followed some blamed Palgrave for failing to defend them. Others spoke darkly of Standish setting things up to make a final killing. By the end of the week the biumverate had been dissolved by popular vote. A third year, Bagnall (or possibly Pagnall), was elected to replace them. He promised weekly assemblies and votes on all collective patrol matters. At the first assembly Palgrave

216

and Standish were unanimously banished to Coventry, irrevocably and eternally. All those possessions of theirs that could be found which had survived the cataclysm of the horse, among them seven flawless wooden drawer-knobs, were distributed among the patrol. But they did not care any more. For they were leaving soon.

the first lesson

Sarah had dropped us at the terminal two hours before take-off but all afternoon delay had followed delay. While Ferrers mooched about buying presents for my parents I stayed close to the departures screen, willing the digits into life. I could see the old MEA 707 waiting out on the tarmac, and the little green cedar tree on its tail, as clipped and neat as something from a topiary. Ferrers kept returning with more gifts, mugs and tea-towels and sugar spoons, all featuring famous landmarks of London. I hadn't the heart to stop him.

We had been told not to leave the campus, but the gateman chewing sunflower seeds only looked up at those coming in. On the streets around Ain Mreisse there was less rubbish burning and the guards sitting outside the shops were no longer wearing masks. We made our way past the tables outside Socrates, taking turns on the Balmoral, the front tyre of which was almost flat. With his dark wiry hair and almond eyes Ferrers didn't stand out much, not like Cooke or Palgrave would have done. When we reached the Lindbergh villa all the shutters were down. The recliners and deck-chairs had gone from the veranda too, but Ferrers noticed the terracotta tiles had recently been swept. I pulled the bell, and after a while one of the shutters upstairs opened and the Druz girl came down and unbolted the door. She was dressed in the Western style now, with flared jeans and a skinny T-shirt. An oily fringe half-covered her eyes. With all the shutters closed it was dark inside, and the rooms smelt of sweat and stale incense. She showed us through to the sitting room which was lit with candles. Trench was laid out in a long white *umbaz* exactly where I had left him, on the divan which had been piled high with every cushion in the house. For the first time he actually looked quite pleased to see me. He even smiled a chink.

'Hey. Welcome home, little man.' He pushed some cushions down from his hill. 'You guys are lucky you got generators on the campus. Try to run a fridge on two hours' power.'

His hair had grown again but was thinning at the front. The Druz girl clambered up and slunk down next to him. He peered down at her, as if she were far away, and his eyes were sunk and rheumy like an old hound-dog.

'Hey. We've got ice! You guys want a Fanta, 7-up? We've got all that stuff.' A sudden charge of animation shook through him. He began to punch the cushions with his fist.

'When the ice melts we bathe in it.'

'Oh really.' Ferrers pretended to sound interested.

'Yeah, man. You open a tap around here and the creature from the swamp crawls out . . . you guys want that iced drink or what?'

'I wondered if you still had the bike?'

'Sure I got it.'

'I hoped we could borrow it for a while.'

'Don't lose it, fuckhead. The kids like those chopper bikes. Remember Batman. He saw his folks shot up when he was seven, right?'

222

'Right?' Ferrers was still trying not to look at Trench.

'Yeah. Right. So those kids didn't turn out like Batman. Comprendez?'

Ferrers recoiled from the chopper so I let him take the Balmoral. When we came out down on the corniche the air was fresher. The sea breeze was carrying the smell of frying *farriden* along the front. We followed the wide promenade, making chicanes of the holes and the old men walking alone clacking their worry beads behind their backs. A little way beyond the empty British Embassy we could see an elderly Syrian T-54, partly covered by tarpaulins, with sandbags to one side of it. It was a hoggish and slothful old tank, like something that had collapsed under its own weight and wasn't going to get up again. As we came closer we saw the soldiers slumped behind the sandbags in their fatigues and jaunty plum berets. They waved and smiled as we cycled by.

There was a touch of the wardrobe about the berets. They were the type that fashionable women wear to radical parties. Ever since I had begun to sow dragon's teeth in the lower gardens I had always imagined the city under the occupation of foreign warriors. Macedonian phalanxes grinding down their enemies like chick peas. Marines fighting their way up the beaches. Dead surfers plundering the souk Ayas. Israeli paratroopers falling thick as ash from a volcano. But never had I imagined this, never Syrian peasants in natty caps from a rue Hamra boutique.

Beyond the tank we began to climb towards the Raoche. The incline was further loosening the front tyre on the Balmoral but Ferrers knew a way of keeping his weight to the back. At the top there were more soldiers in berets standing about outside the fish restaurants and the Kentucky Fried Chicken looking in at the tables. From the promenade we could see down to the Pigeon Rocks where the water-skiers used to show off by gliding through the hole, and beyond the stalled Ferris wheel, like the treadmill of a giant gerbil. I tried to spot the place where the beach house used to be, but there were families living in the huts now and tents pitched between with washing hanging out, and fires burning on the sand.

From the rocks it was an easy ride down. We coasted past Mzeitbeh, past the end of Corniche Mazra. As we continued along the seafront I pointed out the white blocks of flats with their marble hallways where friends of my parents had once lived, oil men and officials from UN-WRA. We passed the skeletons of old building sites, sagging and overgrown, and others where families had built shelters and children played with pie-dogs which barked when they saw the bicycles.

As we turned inwards from the sea towards Fakhani the streets became narrower and crowded with *services* and wheelbarrow men bringing in water-melons and bananas from the south who called up to the pock-marked apartment blocks from which women let down baskets on ropes. The bananas were already going soft in the heat. Some of the wheelbarrow men had parked in the shade beneath the apartments where the breeze-block walls were covered in posters and paintings of suicide martyrs garlanded with tulips and roses, in the background the streams and fountains of paradise. Further up one of the buildings had lost its entire façade. We could see straight into every room as at the ruined house in Hobson Wood. But most of the furniture was still inside. And there were families sitting in silence eating okra and rice under livid pictures of the mosque of Omar, with leather armchairs and brass standard lamps still teetering on the parapet beside them. All the way along the crowded street Ferrers kept asking me to show him which one was Arafat's house so I pointed at the first block we passed and said, 'There. He lives in that one.' Then I told him not to speak loudly any more.

224

Beside the gates into Sabra-Chatila there are some Fatah boys in combat jackets and khakis, hardly older than we are, leaning back against the wall as if they were waiting to catch a bus, their dusty AK47s propped up against their knees. As we come level with them I call out Omer's name, and the oldest who has long hair and a Pepsi T-shirt under his jacket nods us through without looking up. We dismount and walk the bikes down through the sloping alleys. Open sewers run along the middle of the mud pathways but the place smells mostly of dead ants and cat pee. Some of the alleys are so narrow that it is difficult not to wet the bikes. The children playing in the streams with cardboard boats run behind us and touch the wheels, laughing when their hands stick in under the mud-guards. One little boy with crusader-blue eyes and sandy hair tries to slide along grasping the back light of the Balmoral, and the others cling on to the back of his T-shirt and are pulled forward through the mud.

At every major clearing, drinking coffee out of glass cups behind sandbags and on the flat roofs of the larger buildings, there are more Fatah men, and Saiqua units also in camou-flage fatigues, with ammunition belts and *keffiehs*. The Fatah men direct us forward into the clustered hollow of black tin roofs weighted down by rocks and Nido and Crisco tins filled with mud. Here more children are playing where the shelling has levelled the breeze-block huts. After chasing away our splashing train they escort us down into the hollow with their wooden Kalashnikovs.

We passed a long one-storey hall, one wall of which was covered by a mural of the younger Arafat, his stubble faithfully rendered. Inside the martyrs' channel was playing but there was nobody watching. Next to the hall some of the huts had small clay gardens outside, cordoned off by lines of breeze-blocks, and there were Nido tins filled with ger-aniums outside the doors. In the clearing a girl with the face

225

of an old woman was taking water from the pump. While I asked her the way Ferrers stroked the back of her goat as if it were a dog. She smiled at this, and pointed our way down through the close huts.

There were only two chairs in the front room, but Omer's father insisted on standing while Farida, the younger sister, brought honey and *lebneh* and thin mountain bread which she had warmed in the small Butagas oven. When she had placed the food on the low hardboard table she stood behind the plastic-bead curtain which divided the two rooms and watched us eat. Despite the heat Omer's father wore a woollen cap and two ravelled woollen cardigans which came down almost to his knees and furry slippers which he had stuffed with newspaper. After we had finished the warm bread and honey he brought down a faded Groppi Patisserie tin with a picture of the Nile by moonlight on the lid out of which he fished two flaking *burma* pastries, the size of little fingers, unwinding them carefully from a large sheet of tissue. We tried to refuse but he pressed them into our palms. His hands were cool, like stones underground. He watched as Ferrers tried to swallow. 'You like?' He spoke Mandate English, looping, cracked, like an early phonograph recording. 'You like biscuit? Tip-Top Basha biscuit. Since my son lost from Tel al-Za'atar the committee bring much food.' With some effort he kept smiling all the time that he spoke, and yet he seemed faintly shocked to be drawing up these strange syllables out of himself after so many years, as if they were something he had lost long ago down a deep well. When he had finished speaking he straightened his cap and called for Farida to bring coffee for the Bashas.

Old neighbours had begun to gather in the doorway to the alley and behind the plastic curtain. Some had brought their own coffee cups and Farida served them

226

from a brass pot with a long handle. Word of the *Inglisi* had circulated quickly, but only the oldest women, those with toothless mouths and indigo web tattoos on their necks, continued to stare from under their loose linen wimples. Ferrers ignored them and watched the bicycles out in the alley. As the neighbours filed past with their cups, many of them chuckling like children, the old man pointed into the distance, as if they had all been walking by on the other side of a square, and called out their names and the names of the streets where they had once lived. *Allenby. Tawile. Jaffa Road.* They had been neighbours all their lives it seemed, in Lydda, and here too in the camp where the order of the old streets had been retained. Still smiling he looked down at the scraped-out *lebneh* dish and then up again towards the metallic haze over the mountains. As he spoke once more he spat on the concrete floor but all the time he kept his hospitable smile. 'Lubnan.' He paused to draw up the old words. 'Lubnan, Lubnan, land of milk. Bad mother. Dry like deserts.' But Ferrers was not listening to the old man. He had turned his head stiffly towards the inner room. At first I thought it must have been something unusual behind the bead curtain which had caught his eye, a camp official, perhaps, come to check on the visitors. Then I realized he was not looking through the bead curtain, but in front of it, at the old woman with a straight back, taller than the others, who was standing sipping her coffee with her back to the curtain. Her long forearms hardly stirred outside her *izaas* as she lifted the cup to the narrow crevice where her lips had once been; like the other women she sipped her coffee with her mouth, not with the hardened stumps of her lips. On her left forearm she had a tidy rectangular birth mark, no larger than a name tape. Then she passed her cup back through the curtain, and I saw what it was.

As the old man explained the woman appeared not to listen. She gazed out into the alley, at the bicycles standing against the wall. She was used to people talking about her in the third person. And the old man's tone suggested he had told her story not a few times over the years. There was an almost apologetic note in his voice, as if he wished to be excused for telling us that which we already surely knew. *Yes, Mira had been at Dashoo* – as he pronounced it. *After the war Mira had married Hassan Kayed, the handsome carpenter from the Jaffa Road, and in '48 she had fled with her husband and all the others after the massacres.* The way he set it out her presence among them seemed so natural, so given, that immediately I felt foolish and ashamed for having raised the matter, as if I had just made a crude reference to an amputation or a palsy among a gathering of the handicapped, and without thinking what I was saying I began to stumble away into other unrelated subjects in rapid succession: the situation in the south, the humidity, the Silver Jubilee. Tentatively at first, but with growing confidence, as I rambled on, not knowing really who I was addressing any more, not remembering what I had just said, the old women had begun to crowd in a circle around us, blocking out the light from the alley. The hot, strangely perfumed air from inside their jellabas was making it difficult to speak, and difficult to take in breath without gagging. Ferrers was trying to stand up. He had half-closed his eyes. The women were all speaking at the same time. *Did we know her? Did she wear her crown all the time? Was it true that she never went to the bathroom?* Ferrers was forcing his way out now into the alley, pushing aside the ranks of thin robed bodies that stood between him and the light. I reached across and tried to pull him back. In a final effort to break out he dived forwards losing his balance, lurching away . . . Later I found him in the

228

clearing outside the hall where we had met the woman with the goat. He had dropped the Balmoral in the mud and was sitting on a Nido tin, staring at his hands. I tried to explain what the women had been saying. But he turned and hit me in the chest and shouted at the top of his broken voice that I was lying and that he would never believe anything I ever said to him again.

I followed him a little way until he stopped beside the water-pump. Some of the children who had escorted us down had gathered under the hall. Inside the martyrs' channel was playing but the place was empty. Silently they watched us, leaning on their plywood assault rifles.

'What do you mean?' As I spoke he turned round slowly to face me. He seemed startled, in a way I had never seen before, as if an old skin had suddenly fallen from him and his new form emerging through the peeling slough shocked him to the very core. For the first time when he looked into my eyes he did not turn away. He did not seem to have thought what he was going to say. But he began speaking all the same although at first I couldn't hear him clearly. He kept rubbing at one of his eyes and then holding his hand over it. When he lowered the hand his eye was wet and bloodshot.

He spoke slowly, more carefully now. 'You know I used to be an agent for the Duffer when we were juniors. You did know that. But this was all that really mattered. I was prepared to sacrifice . . .' He took his hand down and began pounding it into his thigh until his knuckles went white. Again he looked square at me. He was still speaking but weakly again and I could barely make him out. 'I never expected to see someone like her here . . .'

This time I turned away. I couldn't bear to see his eyes going all soppy for forgiveness like some cringing Jesus-creeper the way they were. I just wanted him to be himself again and to forget what had happened. I began to push the chopper up across the clearing, away from the hall.

We wouldn't have to talk much on the ride home. I felt relieved about that.

I do not know if Ferrers had forgotten about the underground arsenals and the underground shooting-ranges but he did not mention them again. For the rest of his stay we did not leave the campus. He showed little appetite to go spotting Syrian tanks or to search out Fatah men who would let us touch their guns. Nor did he want to stalk snogging students or skateboard on the wide steps down from West Hall. He seemed preoccupied, indifferent to everything I suggested. I would come back to the hammock an hour later and find him still on the same page of Neville Shute. Some days he spent writing long letters which he knew he could not post. In the evenings we stayed up watching American TV shows and he would let me win at chess. When I played old records which my sister had left behind out across the gardens he did not fight or complain.

On the day before he left, in a last attempt to shake him from his torpor, I suggested we dig out the Todarev and go down to the beach and shoot at pigeons and gulls. But when we looked I could not remember exactly where I had buried the polythene bag. The earth in the lower gardens was hard and cracked, and it was difficult to dig down just with sticks. I brought a spade and a seeding-rod up from the tool house. All morning we dug and prodded under the broken swing and under the cedar that did not like the sea. We found gnawed dog's bones and broken glass and black roots, but not a trace of the bag. It was not long before he had lost interest in the search. He began to cover the same ground. He did not even look down at the earth beneath him. I knew then that Ferrers had already begun another dig of his own, the object of which he had not the slightest intention of disclosing, and that there would come a time soon when his sullen perplexities would no longer exert their hold on me.

conflicting reports

I remember little of that first term except the mud and the cold in the dormitories. There was always running over flagstones, somewhere new to report, something else to be late for. In the mornings we learnt about subjunctives and the war poets and in the afternoons we fought for a ball in churning mud between nets of rope. Nobody understood the rules of this game, and nobody explained. At intervals a whistle blew and the scrum would go down and it would all begin again. I was sent to stand outside the nets and throw the ball in. Often I would forget where I was and a master would creep up behind me and blow his whistle. I did not jump up and down to keep warm. Somehow movement made the air keener, and by the time I had reached the showers the water was always cold. Boys from North Hill had a reputation for toughness which I did not uphold.

My dormitory was in the house on St Michael's Road that I had visited the previous summer. I had hoped to find Duff-Revel ruling the place in some style but I was told he had been expelled the term before I arrived, and when boys spoke of it they made the gesture of the hooked wrist. At first

I did not know what this signified and I was ashamed to have to ask. I was given a desk and shelves in the L-shaped hall which, imitating the others, I covered in a tent of safety-pinned curtains and sheets for privacy. These were ripped down so frequently that in the end I stopped bothering to put them up again.

Sometimes I would see Ferrers scuttling across the school courtyard in his black scholar's gowns. He would point up at my straw hat and laugh. There was no time to stop and talk. Anyway it was not done to be seen speaking to collegemen who were all considered mad or queer. Some were said to hang around the bog-houses, offering a fiver to anyone who would go into a cubicle with them. I never saw any there. The bog-houses were always full of smokers and boys doing sketches from Python.

One afternoon I came in late from the fields and the changing rooms were already quiet and almost empty. I crouched down on one of the wooden benches with my head between my knees, too tired to try the showers which I knew would be cold. All over the floor there were lumps of dried mud printed with the studs of boots, and more mud on the hanging shirts which boys wore over and over again without washing. Behind the partition some seniors were telling jokes to each other. *What goes into thirteen twice?* The voice was slow, liturgically measured, as if it had some sacred text to impart. Some of the seniors began chuckling before they heard the punchline, or maybe they had heard it already. *Roman Polanski.* It meant nothing to me but they all snorted and pushed each other around as if it was the funniest name in the world. When they had piped down a little the same voice that had told the joke began to intone, solemnly, almost in plainsong:

> *Charles and Harry,*
> *Charles and Harry,*
> *Go together*
> *Like a horse and carriage . . .*

The words had been changed but I recognized the tune. It was from one of those old records warped by the humid summers that my mother used to play sometimes on the HMV in the long room during siesta hour. *Love and Marriage go together like a horse and carriage/All the something somethings adore it . . .* The seniors were laughing again, not quite so loudly this time. It must have been an insider joke. There was no one in the house known by those names, of that I was almost sure. When he spoke again I remembered the night in the sickbay five years before, perhaps to a day, when I had last heard his voice. As we do more often than we know, when young, I had pledged to myself that I would recall that night again at some remote place in the future. Too prosaic to offer itself as a presentiment exactly, this pledge which presaged nothing but its own remembrance had soon grown dusty and been forgotten. And now, at a moment that could never have been fore-told, that small promise had been redeemed, and yet how many other such wagers, such side-bets against oblivion, would never be redeemed, would prefigure nothing but their own absolute effacement. This was the view from Ferrers' room, the cold fall into dissolution and forgetting. For, despite itself, this doggerel was an oracle of sorts, and I had heard a future which I had yet to understand.

When I thought of Omer I pictured his disappearance as a betrayal of all those reunions which would have spelt the end

237

of the war. By disappearing he had assured me that the war would go on. Since hearing a little of what had happened at Tel al-Za'atar and the Springs of the Pomegranate I had stopped inventing these scenes of reunion and did not wish to begin with them again. Yet despite what Trench had told me about the Phalange with strings of ears on their belts and the still twitching stumps drawn behind *services* I had never doubted the fact of that reunion. I had taken Trench's letters and read them on the plane back but they were all lies and soppy stories about the orphaned cats of Ain Mreisse. Some pages I tore, and the others I did not send.

As the terms went by Ferrers began to slip away from what I had known of him. We did not avoid each other, but nor did we make efforts to meet. Sometimes I would see him walking with a cello in College Street. He strapped it to his back like an *ataal* and went forwards crouching, eyes lowered. Sometimes on summer evenings I would pass him jogging back from Boat Club as I returned from tennis across the water-meadows. He would always grin and wave.

In my second year I joined a group of older boys interested in painting who spent the afternoons taking tea in the conservatory of a large house on College Street which belonged to the art master, an Australian aesthete of independent means. This group went in for double-breasted suits and silk scarves and smoked oval Turkish cigarettes. When the Brideshead thing started they all moved over to black roll-necks and Roland Barthes. Under their influence I began to look at paintings and go to cafés in town with a choice volume clutched to my breast. Ferrers did not frequent these places, nor did I see him in the smoking holes or the pubs in Southgate Street that turned a blind eye. On the whole Collegemen were rarely seen *up town*.

I no longer read the papers and avoided the television. Sometimes my sister would come down in her canary GPO van with crumpled telexes from the Commodore and brown heroin from the Bekaa which made me spew up all the lunch I had bought at the Royal. When she clop-clopped through the study hall in her patent boots boys would give each other hand shandies behind the curtains. I derived a certain reflected glory from these sporadic appearances. Enough at least to ensure that I no longer had to defend myself and could begin to forget about home.

Reprise

David had relaxed again now that he was certain he knew the road. He kept looking out of the window and rubbing his bloodshot eyes, not that there was anything much to see quite yet, just more cars, empty pavements, some women carrying shopping bags across a footbridge. He had stopped following the signs. As we slowed again he was peering between the hoardings, trying to catch the squat tower of the cathedral perhaps, or maybe just something he could recognize.

Once off the ring-road and into the town we worked our way up through the new counter-intuitive one-way system which spilled us out at the bottom of the hill. The Sarum Road had not outwardly altered. Still the hospital, then the prison, then the garden centre. Enough years had passed for it all to look like any other into-town road, Victorian red brick behind too many signs, boring in its own particular way. I had half-expected to find the buildings shuffled into another order, defying my expectations, but there was none of that. It was all so much the same that I barely bothered to look more closely.

Of the school itself little remained except the central section of the building, the brickwork sandblasted and scrubbed into an almost uniform scallop pink. Young men in chain-store suits and hard hats were walking with clipboards up a new macadam drive between transit vans and tidy lines of baby conifers. The walls alone had been preserved by the taxidermist architects, but within there was nothing we would recognize. Airy and open stairwells led past wide reception areas into conference rooms full of unexceptionable Scandinavian furniture. We walked away and round to the back. They had not finished yet with the grounds. The shells of new houses clustered around a network of closes. Grass had been laid down and shrubs planted in front of the show house. Through the window we could see a suite in Navaho prints, a walnut coffee table, magazines neatly fanned out.

At the back of the estate the grass was long and stiff with frost. Links of damp cord marked a boundary between the last close and the fields beyond. As David lifted the cord it dropped and disappeared in the long grass, like something sinking into dark water. We walked out, over the cold untrodden ground. At the bottom of the fields the bank with the horse-chestnuts above it had not been disturbed. Where the grass was shortest we clambered up, pushing our way through the overgrown hedge at the top. It was difficult to make out where the paths had once been. The weeds were thick and the paving stones had gone. The pond was still there though, drained and strangely perfect in its empty symmetry. For some moments we shuffled about in the hollow hemisphere with the darkness coming in behind us as it always had, in over the fields and the horizon we no longer recognized with all its factitious melancholy. As we climbed out David looked back over the smooth crater towards the place where the war memorial and the statue had once been. He had not gone across to see. He walked on ahead while in the distance, on the other side of the fields, yellow and orange hard hats bobbed festively beneath the fine tracing of the scaffolding and the shells of the houses.

On our way out we stopped off for tea at the Royal. The view from the conservatory across the croquet lawn had been sacrificed to a new annexe, but the service had improved. David had begun to tell me about his recent trip to Vancouver. He had some theory about the Pacific – how it marked the finitude of the West as an idea, or some such – I don't know if he really expected me to be paying attention. We did not meet often now (his family and his work) and when we did it was never to discuss the one matter that still bound us together. Whenever, increasingly infrequently, I would meet, by chance, or by choice, any of the others they would certainly be candid and voluble in ways they surely could not be with their more regular friends, and yet none of them would ever make reference back to our common life and what we still shared from those years. (Sometimes X or Y would occasion the sobriquet *in –'s year at school*, or there would be the qualification *I think – might have been at school with us*, but such allusions only served to legitimate the wilful negation of reminiscence and deepen it.) I had not attempted to breach this unwritten covenant of silence, and I could not explain to myself why I had not. And I believe it was for this reason and no other that I set about writing a chronicle of those years.

All the more surprising then that David should have undertaken this sentimental journey. He had been aware of my intentions at the outset. I had not tried to conceal them from him, as I had from the others. And yet he made no further reference to the project. Possibly he considered the idea of such a chronicle fanciful, or simply irrelevant to what he had become. We had only met again by chance. After leaving we had not kept up. Seven years had passed without contact on either side. Then in the February of '88 we had found ourselves seated together, one empty place between us, on the last flight back from Geneva. David had been spending the weekend at Davos with a colleague from Basle whom I would meet later at the wedding. It had been my third connection of the day. I was dog-tired and slightly feverish after the long wait in Amman and the morning drive past the camps. At first David had not looked up. I had this crazy notion that when I spoke he would claim to be someone else. As the minutes went by this had come to seem like a certainty and I began to wonder whether I should believe him when he gave another name. By the time the hostess brought the cashew nuts he had fallen asleep.

The night before I had seen Trench off on to the Larnaca boat at Jounieh. It had not been safe for him to go out through the western sector and take the airport road. When I picked him up at the villa he was pinned and still limping from the operation. I had grown accustomed to meeting and touching the grey un-sunned flesh of those who had not been out in years (it was beautiful in its way) but I had seen nothing like this: it was as if his whole body had been in plaster for decades. Wars are honey pots for junkies: so many heavy painkillers and so little regulation; for years the chemists of Ain Mreisse had been servicing his habits, supplying him with pethidine, Tuinal, Seconal – the works. When they operated none of the anaesthetics had even touched him. The doctors at the AUB hospital said they had never seen a man in such pain. On the quay he had suddenly grabbed my hand and tried to pull me back towards the broken road. He was crawling on the ground and scratching at his face. He had begged me again and again to let him stay. In the end I had given one of the Phalange a hundred dollars to mind him at the other end. The Phalange was holding him from behind as I ran back across the quay, threatening to throw him into the sea if he had any more trouble from him; perhaps he wanted to let me know I was going to get my money's worth.

When David had woken as we were descending and saw me sitting next to him he thought it was a great joke. He immediately ordered champagne and then sent it back when it came in plastic bottles. His ears were still plugged with wax balls and for a while we had some difficulty understanding each other. At some point during the descent I had enquired if he had read any reports on the battles in the camps; at home I never read the papers or watched television. It was then that he had asked me about Mira. At first I could not think who he was talking about.

'Fine, she's fine,' I said, until he reminded me. Naturally I was curious to know why he had remembered the name after so long.

'Who knows?' He was looking away as he spoke, down the aisle where nobody was standing. 'Perhaps because it was my grandmother's name.'

The fact of Mira's death, of course, was indeterminate yet certain. If she had survived the massacres she would have been buried in one of the underground cemeteries. I smiled and told him she had escaped to Australia: with Omer's little sister Farida who was now working with MCI Communications in Sydney. This at least was miraculously true. David visibly relaxed when he heard the news and decided on the champagne after all. After we landed he had insisted on driving me in from Heathrow and refused to let me return to my empty flat. At the house on Frognal Hill Rachel was waiting in a little black dress with the glass table laid for two and more champagne on ice. They would be married in the summer.

By the time we left the Royal many of the other tables had filled up with boys. The darkness outside made everything in the room seem suddenly brighter, larger. The boys were sharing coffees and posing with paperbacks and smoking from cigarette holders. Some of them wore black roll-necks, and others double-breasted suit jackets and white silk scarves: the clothes did not fit well, but they never had. The props, the setting, the staging, had remained the same, though of course the original cast had long moved on to other work, to other roles in other cities throughout the world. These were the understudies of understudies, a tourist act. Still, it was nice to see the show running after all these years.